SEE HER VANISH

(A Mia North FBI Suspense Thriller—Book 4)

Rylie Dark

Rylie Dark

Bestselling author Rylie Dark is author of the SADIE PRICE FBI SUSPENSE THRILLER series, comprising six books (and counting); the MIA NORTH FBI SUSPENSE THRILLER series, comprising six books (and counting); the CARLY SEE FBI SUSPENSE THRILLER, comprising six books (and counting); and the MORGAN STARK FBI SUSPENSE THRILLER, comprising three books (and counting).

An avid reader and lifelong fan of the mystery and thriller genres, Rylie loves to hear from you, so please feel free to visit www.ryliedark.com to learn more and stay in touch.

ISBN: 978-1-0943-9515-9

BOOKS BY RYLIE DARK

SADIE PRICE FBI SUSPENSE THRILLER
ONLY MURDER (Book #1)
ONLY RAGE (Book #2)
ONLY HIS (Book #3)
ONLY ONCE (Book #4)
ONLY SPITE (Book #5)
ONLY MADNESS (Book #6)

MIA NORTH FBI SUSPENSE THRILLER
SEE HER RUN (Book #1)
SEE HER HIDE (Book #2)
SEE HER SCREAM (Book #3)
SEE HER VANISH (Book #4)
SEE HER GONE (Book #5)
SEE HER DEAD (Book #6)

CARLY SEE FBI SUSPENSE THRILLER
NO WAY OUT (Book #1)
NO WAY BACK (Book #2)
NO WAY HOME (Book #3)
NO WAY LEFT (Book #4)
NO WAY UP (Book #5)
NO WAY TO DIE (Book #6)

MORGAN STARK FBI SUSPENSE THRILLER
TOO LATE (Book #1)
TOO CLOSE (Book #2)
TOO FAR GONE (Book #3)

CHAPTER ONE

Lookout Point, on one of the few bluffs overlooking Dallas, was the perfect spot for making out.

Or at least, it would've been, if Sadie McIntosh hadn't been utterly alone.

She sucked on her strawberry-flavored e-cigarette, hoping to calm her nerves, and looked down at her cell phone display. No messages.

Why was she vaping? Her mom told her it put holes in her lungs. That's why she only did it when she was stressed about something. Thinking of her mom, she willed herself to put the cigarette away.

Instead, she took another puff, then she looked down the lane, hoping to see the headlights of his old Jeep, cutting through the darkness. But there was nothing. There were cars parked all around her, but most of them were silent, some rocking slightly, windows steamed.

No one cared that she was there.

Not even Mike. *Especially* not him.

Sadie sighed. Weren't all seventeen-year-olds supposed to be desperate for it? And here, she'd been dangling it in front of him. *Constantly* mentioning, all last week, that she was planning to come here and take in the view. Alone. Hint, hint. All he had to do was reach out and take it.

But did he ever? Nope. They'd been hanging out for almost a month, and she'd never met anyone so cold.

Maybe he's gay, her friends had said. But she'd told them no, not possible. He was into her. He'd said it, several times. And tonight was supposed to prove it. She told him where she'd be, had Natalie drive her up here on her way to work, and . . . nothing.

Maybe her friends were right.

Sighing, she walked in the darkness for a little while, past the cars, her sneakers filling with stones. He thought he could stand her up? No. She'd break up with him. That would show him. Not that they were *together*, together. But now, she'd make it known, in no uncertain terms, that it would never happen. She'd make sure there was a big scene at high school on Monday, and he'd beg for forgiveness. And ha—she wouldn't give it to him.

The thought cemented in her head as she walked, until her phone dinged.

She pulled it up, excited to find the text from him. *Sorry, babe. Still want to meet you. Running a little late.*

She scowled, then jumped onto the top of an old picnic table and quickly thumbed in: *A little late? I've been waiting for a half-hour!*

A moment later, the text came up: *I'm doing the best I can.*

She thumbed in: *Do better.*

His next text came all too quickly: *Screw this. I don't need you on my back. I'm going to hang out with my boys.*

She stared at it, the words burning themselves into her retinas, her fingers shaking. Then she punched in: *FINE!*

Seething, now, she shoved her phone into the pocket of her jeans and hopped down from the table. Off in the distance, the lights of downtown Dallas were shining, bright and colorful, like fireworks. She turned away, facing the full moon, which was drifting higher in the sky. Around her, the rooftops of the cars shone in the pale moonlight. Inside them, people were together, enjoying one another, in love.

And she was alone.

"Michael Masterson, I frigging hate you," she snarled under her breath, shoving her vaping pen into her bag and taking off in a run.

When she reached the edge of the parking lot, she saw the orange-lit tips of a couple cigarettes. A voice called, "Hey, Sadie, that you?"

Oh, no. It was those losers from her gym class, the ones who always ogled her in her short shorts. What were they doing out here?

She reversed direction and headed straight into the woods, branches and brambles slapping her face and bare legs. She didn't care. She just wanted to get away from everyone that had anything to do with her high school. One year. One more year, and she could graduate, go to college, and never look back again.

Behind her, she heard a branch crack.

They were following her.

Hadn't Natalie told her that this was a stupid idea? She'd ignored her best friend, because she'd wanted Mike so much. She'd played this night over and over again in her mind, imagined him kissing her, touching her, wanting her, fueled by love scenes from her favorite movies. She'd built it up so much in her mind that she felt sure it would be everything she dreamed of. But now, she felt like a total fool.

A total fool who was now in some serious danger.

A male laugh erupted behind her, startlingly close. Swallowing, Sadie picked up the pace and ran into a clearing. The earth underneath her feet was uneven, full of muddy ruts. Her sneakers sank into it.

"Thanks, Mike, you've ruined my favorite Vans," she muttered bitterly, running across the field, wanting to leave everything and everyone behind.

She was running so fast that she didn't notice what was right in front of her until her foot caught on it. She went flying, face first, to the ground. The mud that she'd been so disgusted by proved to be her saving grace, because it cushioned her fall. Her knees and palms hit it first, sinking in.

For a moment, she just froze there, on her hands and knees, staring at the matted grass and breathing in its earthy smell. She was so preoccupied by the notion that if anyone from school saw her they'd be laughing at her, that at first, she didn't care what had caused her to trip.

But then, she realized the smell of earth was mixed with something else. Something sickeningly sweet and foul. It smelled like an animal had died.

And her feet were tangled in something stringy and wet that reminded her of her horse Blue's mane when she rode him in the rain. But this was cold and sticky, a most unpleasant sensation, wrapping around her bare ankles.

Grimacing, she slowly rose to her feet and turned back, reluctant. She expected to see mangled, bloody fur. A poor, dead animal, lying on its side in the mud.

But what she saw was far beyond anything she could have ever imagined.

Blonde hair, pale, green-tinged skin with the pallor of death. A silver cuff on one arm. Not just one body but two, entwined together in some kind of sick love knot, where it was impossible to tell whose arms and legs belonged to whom.

Turning away, she rushed on, trying to put distance between herself and the ghastly sight. Moments later, when her mind fully digested what she'd seen, she finally stopped, heart beating like mad.

And she screamed so loud into the night that all of Lookout Point heard.

CHAPTER TWO

If it's the last thing I do, I'm going to make sure Wilson Andrews goes down.

Mia North sat in the front seat of her beater car, in almost full darkness save for the dim blue light from the digital clock on the dash, repeating that mantra to herself as she waited for her partner to arrive. She'd been repeating those words for months, ever since the Senate hopeful had framed her for murder.

And yet, here she was, still skulking around. Still on the lam. Still away from her family and her life.

And it's all his goddamn fault.

She closed her eyes and listened to a soft Patsy Cline tune on the radio, trying to calm herself. Getting angry didn't help anyone. She'd only make rash decisions, take chances. And now, more than ever, with that U.S. Marshal on not only her tail but the tails of all the people she knew and loved, she had to be careful.

She snorted. *I'm the queen of rash decisions. That's probably what got me into this mess in the first place.*

She straightened as a pair of headlights cut through the darkness, pulling into the abandoned auto repair shop.

It was him. David Hunter. Her partner.

She sighed. *Former* partner. It had been a long time since she'd been a badge-bearing member of the FBI, but it was still a part of her. She still considered herself to be an FBI agent, even if she'd been stripped of the badge. Her entire life had been taken away on the day she was arrested for the murder of child predator Ellis Horvath. As she watched David's car pull into the lot, thoughts of that night came back to her.

She'd acted rashly, barreling into the empty warehouse without waiting for David. But she'd had a good reason. Ellis had been stalking her daughter, Kelsey, and she'd received a call from him, luring her to the place. She wanted to confront him, once and for all.

And then she'd found him there, shot dead.

By whom, she didn't know. She hadn't seen the real culprit.

But Mia had been the perfect patsy. She had motive, opportunity, means . . .

And that bastard Wilson Andrews knew it. He'd done it to cover his serial-killer brother's tracks and conceal what he knew so that he could rise to the state Senate, ruining her life in the process.

But finding a way to bring a man with so much power and influence to his knees wasn't easy. She kept running into roadblocks, wherever she turned. The Andrews behemoth owned a lot of the city, paid many people off. That she'd survived this long, without being caught, was a virtual miracle. Every time she uncovered a new piece of the puzzle, it only served to show her how enormous and complicated the puzzle really was.

This time, though, she had a slight lead.

His name was Ernie Modesto, and he was a hitman that Wilson Andrews had hired to kill Kevin Reynolds, the police officer she thought might have actually killed Ellis Horvath. She'd stumbled upon Kevin's dead body. She'd seen money change hands between Andrews and Modesto. She knew Andrews deserved to be in prison, not her. She just needed a gotcha.

Easier said than done.

Mia watched as David Hunter parked his car and stepped out. Looking both ways, he went to the busted night drop box, and slipped something inside.

Then, just as quietly as he'd come, he got back into his car and took off.

After his car took off toward the highway, its taillights disappearing in traffic, she watched him go, wishing she could say something to him. This lonely life meant that she hadn't spoken to anyone in days, not since she left the motel on the border where her husband Aiden had surprised her for a quick hug and kiss. But any more than that was impossible. She was almost totally cut off from everyone she cared about.

She waited there for a minute, two, thinking about that case on the border. It'd been a misogynistic cult that she'd infiltrated and brought down, with the help of her sister, Francine. It was a good thing, a reminder that she could have a positive effect on the world, even while in hiding.

But it wasn't enough. She missed Francine. She missed Aiden. She missed her daughter, Kelsey. Her heart physically ached at the thought of them.

She sat there in the darkness, then dragged her hands down her face and said a little prayer that whatever information David had for her, it would bring her closer to proving her innocence.

Then she stepped out of the car.

Looking around to make sure she wasn't being followed, she opened the lid on the drop box and pulled out a thin envelope. Very thin. That disappointed her. She wanted volumes of information. So much information that the answers would be obvious.

Then she hurried back to her car, got inside, and sped off to another location, the back of a Whataburger restaurant. She'd learned that the trick of being on the lam was to never spend too long in any one place, and she'd never been to this restaurant before.

Parked by the dumpsters, she looked around once again to make sure no one was near; then she tore open the envelope.

There were a few crisp twenties in there, which she appreciated because she couldn't exactly use her credit card and she'd nearly run out of money, several times. She pocketed them quickly, then unfolded the single sheet of paper and stared at the message:

No dice on Ernie Modesto. Can't find any evidence to tie him to Kevin Reynolds's murder. Modesto has a rap sheet for burglary and assault, but nothing else. Also, looking into mention of any "girl" in Reynolds's history. I'm trying to get a list of Reynolds's past cases this year, and will keep digging, but it's hard, all eyes on me. It's looking pretty grim.

She let out a groan. There was supposed to be more. Ernie had told her that before he'd killed Kevin Reynolds, the officer had mentioned having regrets about some girl. *"He begged for his life like a little sissy. Then he said something about a girl. How he should've come forward back then, when he first found out about it. He kept saying that, over and over again, how he regretted it."*

Found out about what? What did he regret? Her only hope was that whatever it was, it was related to Wilson Andrews, and because Kevin had witnessed it, he'd paid the price of his life. Wilson Andrews was the lowest of the low, despite his skyrocketing popularity and the media saying he could do no wrong. She wouldn't put it past him to have a relationship with some underage girl, then bury it along with everyone who knew about it.

If only she could find the thread. That one thread to pick on, to pull, which would unravel the whole thing. She'd been hoping that a background check on Ernie and Kevin Reynolds would bring a link to the Horvath case that she'd been framed for. But this . . . this felt like a dead end. David would keep digging . . . but with all eyes on him, what else could he do?

She turned the paper over and saw another message he'd scribbled there, in his terrible handwriting.

If you need to get any other info to me, leave it there. I'll check in every few days.

That was something. A little lifeline.

But it wasn't enough. If she was going to find out what really happened the night Ellis Horvath was killed and she was framed, she was going to have to try harder. Dig more into Reynolds's past and who this girl was, on her own.

And, like she'd been doing for the past few months, she'd have to take the bull by the horns herself.

CHAPTER THREE

That morning, after driving the night aimlessly, head swarming with thoughts, Mia pulled into the parking lot of a diner in Ferris, a town south of Dallas.

Right now, her only job was to lay low, and to let David continue his research into Kevin Reynolds's past and the girl he was talking about before his death. But she'd never been good about sitting back and letting other people take the reins.

The only problem was, she'd been driving all night, and she still couldn't think of any way to help her situation. She didn't have access, so she couldn't dive through the files and see what previous cases Reynolds had been working on. She couldn't go back to his apartment, as by now, it'd likely been cleared out. No, she was totally at David's mercy, this time.

So much for taking the bull by the horns. She felt like she was still stuck in the corral.

Sitting in the lot of the run-down diner, she grabbed her wallet and counted out her money. Thankfully, Francine had given her several hundred dollars to tide her over, and with David's cash, her wallet was pretty flush. Still, since she wasn't sure when she'd see a friendly face again, she had to make it last.

As she walked to the entrance of the diner, a man in a cowboy hat was coming out. As he held the door open for her, the smell of bacon and coffee hit her, and her stomach growled. She hadn't eaten in over twenty-four hours.

"Howdy, ma'am," the cowboy said. Though his greeting was friendly, she couldn't shake the feeling that he was staring at her.

"Hi," she said, head tilted down.

Another man came through, too, and was he staring at her, also?

I'm just being paranoid, she told herself. It was a familiar feeling, especially now that she knew the manhunt for her had intensified. She reminded herself that she was fine, that she was careful to never go to the same place twice, to keep herself disguised and cover her tracks, but as she stepped through the door, the feeling remained.

At first, she thought of bolting, going somewhere else, just in case. But her growling stomach won out. She reached into her pocket, pulled out a quarter, and grabbed a copy of the *Dallas Metro News.* If nothing else, she could bury her nose in that.

She went into the diner and took a seat in the back corner of the restaurant, in the most out-of-the-way place she could find. When the waitress arrived, she ordered a large coffee and her bacon and eggs platter, and lifted the newspaper up as a shield between her and the outside world.

As she flipped through the pages, she saw it: *Senate Hopeful Wilson Andrews Meets with Human Rights Coalition.*

She groaned at the photograph of him, standing with a group of well-dressed individuals. They were holding up their linked hands in a victory stance.

She desperately wanted to give him the finger. His face was so rigid, so plastic, it was hard to believe that the poll numbers showed him ten percentage points ahead of the nearest competitor. Couldn't they see what a phony he was?

Apparently, the answer was no. And that number was only trending upward. It'd taken a dip a few weeks ago, when Jerry Andrews, his brother, had been arrested for several murders. But after that? The sky was the limit.

I hate you, she thought, but turned the page. Staring eye-daggers at his photograph wasn't going to give her the results she needed, which was Wilson Andrews, finally exposed for all of his misdeeds. She needed *action.*

But until David Hunter gave her something, her hands were tied.

Breathing out a long sigh, she flipped the page just as the waitress came with her coffee. "You all right, Honey?" the grandmotherly lady said with a smile.

She realized her teeth were clenching. "Uh, yes. Thank you."

"All right. Your breakfast will be out in a minute. You let me know if you need anything, now, all right, Honey?"

She nodded and brought the coffee to her lips. It was too hot to taste, so she just inhaled, letting it calm her nerves.

Mia set it down in the saucer and stared at an article at the top of the local news section.

YOUNG COUPLE FOUND DEAD APPEARS TO BE DOUBLE HOMICIDE

North Dallas police are still investigating a shooting that left a man and a woman dead in a North Dallas field last week.

In the evening hours of this past Saturday, Jason Delaney-Sawyer and Kiki Redbone, both 18, of University Park were found dead from a gunshot wound at the North Dallas Fairgrounds.

While no arrests have been made and no suspects have been publicly named, North Dallas Police Chief Scott Tomkins said investigators believe the two victims knew one another and it is possible that multiple shooters were involved in their slaying.

"Our leads are getting stronger," Tomkins said.

"He was so young," Delaney's aunt, Marsha Delaney, said. "Our family is forever torn apart."

The North Dallas Fairgrounds are located roughly half a mile off Charson Loop Road, behind a large field and down a gravel road across the street from a place called Lookout Point, a popular congregation spot for teenagers.

Tomkins said officers responded after the couple were located by a teenager who called police around 10:42 p.m. Both victims were dead when law enforcement arrived at the scene, he said.

Mia stared at the name of the victim. Delaney-Sawyer.

Now why did that name sound familiar?

In a rush, it came to her.

Linda Delaney-Sawyer. Carolann's mom.

Carolann had been—and maybe still was—Kelsey's best friend in the third grade. Mia hadn't had much time to concern herself with all things High Point Elementary School, but she remembered Linda Delaney-Sawyer well; of all the mothers who'd been at Back to School Night on that first day of first grade, Linda had been the most outgoing and welcoming. She'd invited Kelsey over to a sleepover, at least once a month.

Mia and Linda had immediately hit it off, going out for drinks now and then. As a mother of a teen, Linda was a more experienced parent. Mia liked her no-nonsense, down-to-earth approach to everything. She didn't put on airs, showing off the latest fashions or the nicest car in the parking lot. She wasn't fake. She was real, and easy to get along with.

Plus, she loved her kids. Her blue eyes had shone as she spoke of them and all the activities they were involved in. She loved Carolann, but Linda had also spent a lot of time talking about Jason, and how he was planning to go off to college in a few years, maybe to SCAD, for art, since he was a talented painter.

But now poor Jason was dead. What had happened?

Mia couldn't help thinking of Kelsey, and what it would be like to lose her. How awful. Poor Linda had to have been beside herself.

For so long, Mia had thought that her own situation, being away from family and constantly on the run, was the worst. But now, here was a woman dealing with an even bigger nightmare.

Mia's heart went out to her. She read the article again and again, a fire growing hotter inside her, each time. *Lookout Point. I know that place. It's a big place for teens.*

And trouble, apparently, too.

She had a momentary thought of *What is the world coming to?* This world, where the safest, most benign places were now no longer safe. Where evil could run wild, unchecked, and the good were the ones under attack. Something about all of this was so backwards.

She read the article again.

No suspects.

It was bad enough to find out your son had been murdered and dumped in a field. But to learn the killer was still at large? Never knowing whether the killer would ever be found or brought to justice, or if he'd kill again? That was even worse.

And they were so young. Barely children, probably seniors in high school. It didn't say so, but maybe they'd been dating, and had gone up to this Lookout Point. But what happened? How had they both wound up dead? Had they come across the wrong people in that shadowy area and ruffled feathers?

Mia's mind automatically went to the usual suspects—drugs, gangs. But Linda always had a tight leash on her kids. During the couple of nights they'd gone out for drinks, Mia remembered Linda constantly texting her oldest to keep tabs on him.

More and more questions piled up in her head.

No, Mia certainly wasn't in a place to investigate this. It could be too dangerous.

But then again, she'd been able to slip on and off the radar and solve a number of cases, before. Maybe she could do the same here, to pass the time while waiting for David to get back to her?

She pulled the newspaper down and realized that the waitress had brought her food. She grabbed a fork and took a bite of the hash browns. They were cold. How long ago had the food been delivered to her? And had she been so absorbed in this story that she hadn't noticed?

Big problem. She couldn't let her guard down. All it would take would be one person to recognize her, and the game would be over. She had to keep both eyes open, all the time.

She looked around suspiciously, but no one was watching her.

Breathing a sigh of relief, she dug into her cold plate and finished her breakfast, all the while thinking about the case of Jason Delaney-Sawyer.

It wouldn't hurt to just drop by Linda's neighborhood and scope it out, would it?

CHAPTER FOUR

Linda Delaney-Sawyer's home was in an area about a mile from Mia's neighborhood, on the other side of the highway in University Park. As Mia drove the familiar streets, hood up, sunglasses on, looking out for police cars, she fought the deep urge to turn into her development and stop at her old house.

Aiden and Kelsey wouldn't be there, anyway. It was mid-day, and they were likely at work and school.

School. Mia's heart pinged with longing as she drove past the one-story brick building, Park Elementary School. She could just imagine her nine-year-old daughter, in her fourth grade classroom, sitting behind a desk. Her hair probably wouldn't be in braids—that was far too difficult for Aiden to manage. And no pigtails—even when Mia had been in her life, those were far too babyish for her daughter. So she envisioned her hair in a ponytail, reading a book, maybe raising her hand to answer the teacher's question.

Or maybe it was recess? She slowed down as she passed the building, trying to see if there were any kids out on the playground. But it was too early.

Sighing, she turned back just in time, because the car in front of her had come to a stop. She jammed on her brakes, lurching forward and stopping inches from its back bumper, then let out a sigh of relief. The last thing she needed was to get into a fender-bender now.

Finally, she pulled up to the small white ranch with the black shutters. As she idled there, wondering if she was really going to do this, her mind filled with memories of happier times—taking Kelsey to the front door with a pink sleeping bag and pillow bigger than she was, watching the girls play with water guns in the front yard.

She swallowed. Kelsey might not have had her mother, but she was still living her life, as best she could. Poor Jason was gone.

Making the decision, Mia cut the engine and stepped out onto the curb, then rushed across the lawn, making sure no neighbors were watching. Then she lifted the knocker and let it fall, once, twice.

Immediately, the door opened, and a woman peered out. At first, her dark-ringed, bloodshot eyes were those of a stranger, but gradually, Mia saw bits of the woman she remembered—the blonde hair, now tied back in a ponytail, the slim, statuesque figure. "Linda?" Mia asked.

"Oh, Mia," she said, opening the door wider. She brought a hand to her face and immediately began to cry.

Mia stepped inside and wrapped the woman in a hug. "I heard about it. I am so sorry," she said. "Is there anything I can do?"

She continued to sob into Mia's shoulder for a moment, but then sniffed heavily and wiped at her tears, straightening. "I'm sorry. I'm trying to be strong. For Carolann, you know," she said, looking back, likely to see if her younger child had seen her break down.

Mia smiled, expecting that Linda would ask about her escape, since it was all over the news. The next time she spoke, her voice was stronger. "Please, come in. I was just making lunch. Can I interest you? Tuna salad. Nothing special."

"Thanks, that would be great," Mia said, following her through the house, past many composite pictures featuring the honey-haired boy. She paused for a second at a graduation photo of a kid with hair in his eyes, cap and gown, a lopsided smile.

Poor kid, she thought, hurrying to catch up to Linda. She found her at a small, L-shaped kitchen with dark cabinets, spreading tuna onto Wonder bread. "Carolann! Lunch is ready!" she called, placing a sandwich on a plate.

The little girl came plodding down the stairs in bare feet and flowered shorts, her waist-length, shiny blonde hair bouncing behind her. She eyed Mia cautiously as she took her sandwich and a Snapple. "Thanks, Momma," she said quietly.

Linda smoothed her hair. "You remember Mrs. North, don't you? Kelsey's mom? Say hello."

She nodded. "Hello."

"All right," Linda said, nudging her off. "You can eat in the living room, in front of the television, if you want."

The little girl scurried off as fast as her feet would carry her. Linda set a Snapple in front of Mia and brought two plates over, shaking her head. "It's a shame we lost touch after I moved Carolann to the arts charter school. What's new with you?"

Mia stared, dumbfounded. Was it possible she didn't know? Or was she so beside herself with grief that she'd forgotten. "Well . . . you know . . . you've probably seen the reports . . . the trial . . ."

She shook her head. “Oh, darlin’, I don’t follow the news. I told you that. And I especially don’t, now. Now that Jason’s face is plastered all over it.”

So she didn’t know. With the way people talked about everything, and as friendly as Linda was, it was shocking that she hadn’t heard the gossip. Or maybe she’d ignored it. “I was surprised there was no media outside.”

“Oh, they were out there.” She stared at her sandwich, then set it down. “I told them if they didn’t get the hell out of here, I was going to kill them.”

“That worked?” Mia asked doubtfully.

“It did. I was holding a shotgun when I told them that.” She motioned to the sandwich. “Dig in. Is Kelsey enjoying school? Maybe we should try to get the kids together for a sleepover. I’m sure Carolann would love it.”

Mia nodded. “Kelsey would, too.” She bit into her sandwich. “I’m sure you must be busy with everything. Have the police been around?”

“Yes,” she stared at her sandwich. “I was there the day after it happened, questioned up and down. I just don’t understand how a tragedy like this could happen. Not to Jason. He was such a good boy.”

“Was he dating the girl?”

She nodded. “Kyrie. But she went by Kiki. Popular, all-American, beautiful. From a good family that lived right near your place. The Redbones?” She raised an eyebrow as if to ask Mia if she knew the family, but Mia shook her head. “They’d been dating a few months. Planned to go to University of Texas at Dallas together this fall. They were so happy about it.”

“I see,” Mia said. “It’s certainly a tragic thing. Where were they headed when it happened? Do you know?”

“They were just going out,” she said softly. “They liked to go on drives, go to the diner, watch a movie, that kind of thing. So I thought nothing of it. He’s a momma’s boy, so he texts me all the time, to tell me where he is, or just that he loves me. When he didn’t, after a few hours, I knew something was wrong. I was frantic when he didn’t show up by that morning. I got with Elle Redbone, Kiki’s mom, and found out she was missing, too. We didn’t think they’d run away; they wouldn’t do that. So we called and called, everyone who knew them. No one had seen them. No one at all. It wasn’t until the following night, when I was getting ready for bed, that I got the call. And I just knew he was dead.”

Mia shuddered at the thought of receiving a phone call like that. How awful. She didn't think she'd have half the composure her friend had. She was trying to be strong for her younger daughter, and as far as Mia could see, succeeding. Mia had to give her credit for that. "I'm so sorry."

Linda reached for her phone on the table. She opened it up and pulled up a photograph. "Here. Here it is. The last photo he posted on his Instagram. It was the night he died."

She stared at it. The couple seemed so happy, faces squished together, giving looks that almost seemed invincible. She was giving a peace sign. Beyond that, there was nothing but darkness, the faint black line of treetops against a midnight blue sky. The caption underneath said, #rockinandrollin. "Where are they? At a concert?"

Linda shook her head. "I couldn't tell you. He never told me where they were going, exactly. But they were together. And happy."

"Did they say if they had any suspects?"

For a moment, Linda looked like she might cry again, but then she turned to the living area, where Carolann had gone, and blinked clarity into her eyes. "No. None at all. And you know I asked them. I'm on them constantly, asking if there are developments. They've got nothing. Zero. They're just all bozos. Awful. Rats, running around, chasing their own tails, asking the same questions over and over and never getting anywhere."

Mia fell silent, thinking, but suddenly, Linda gasped.

She reached forward and put a hand on Mia's forearm. "Oh, my gosh, I'm so sorry. I forgot. Aren't you something with law enforcement? I forget . . . "

Mia nodded. "It's all right. I don't—"

She tilted her head. "Wait, aren't you FBI?"

"I was, but—"

"Then you can look into this for me, can't you?" she asked, her eyes pleading. She clapped her hands together in prayer. "Oh, please. This would be such a help to me. You don't know what I have to deal with, with those idiots. If I can get an actual Fed on the case, I'd—"

"I really want to. Unfortunately," Mia said, her heart twisting, "I can't. You see, I have to—"

"Oh, but you have an in as an FBI agent! They'll listen to you!" she said, her eyes wide, her hands now clasped in front of her, shaking.

"I'm not FBI anymore," Mia said. It was the truth.

"You're not?" Linda let out a big sigh, her shoulders slumping. "But you at least have know-how. You can look into it, maybe not officially, and see what you turn up. Right?"

Mia shook her head. "If I interfere with the police . . ." *I'll be arrested and sent to jail for the rest of my life.*

"I'm not asking you to do anything illegal. Just . . . a little snooping around, maybe at the place where the bodies were found? Or I can give you a list of their friends, and—"

"I'm sorry," she said, setting her half-eaten sandwich down and standing up. "As much as I want to help, I really can't. But I did want to come by and offer my condolences."

Linda's face fell. "Oh. Yes. Well, thank you. I'll see you to the door, then."

Mia walked to the door and, as much as she tried to avoid it, her eyes caught on a picture of a younger Jason, in front of a beach, with his family. He was smiling in braces, but his eyes seemed to beg Mia for help. *Poor kid,* she thought again. *Someone needs to find his killer.*

She took another step, and another voice spoke inside her. *Why not you?*

She gritted her teeth. *Because, the more I look into these crimes, the closer I'm putting myself to the police and the people who want to apprehend me. And I've been lucky so far, but if I keep tempting fate, my luck is going to run out.*

She turned back to Linda. "Could you please not tell anyone I was here?"

Linda lifted an eyebrow.

"I'm supposed to be on another case. If they find out I was here, they'll come down on me," she explained.

"Oh. Of course," the woman said, twisting her hands. "I appreciate you stopping by."

She said goodbye to Linda, who barely looked at her, now, making her feel even guiltier. Every muscle inside Mia wanted her to go ahead and look into this case. But she couldn't. She couldn't take that chance. What she needed to do was stay in hiding, and figure out a solution to her own problem with Wilson Andrews. Not play around with new ones.

CHAPTER FIVE

U.S. Marshal Kane Wilcox ran a hand through his scrubby hair, which was damp with sweat from the hot desert sun, beating down upon his scalp. Then he climbed into his car and turned up the AC as far as it would go. He'd be happy to get out of this hellhole.

The Rising Sun commune was, as far as he was concerned, the pit of hell. He'd been here for the past three days, hot on the heels of former FBI Agent Mia North. Or at least, he'd *thought* he'd been hot on her heels.

Now, though, he had a feeling it was just the desert sun, playing games with him.

The trail was cold. She'd escaped him, yet again.

He looked over at the pile of junk on the front passenger seat, pulling out a blue flannel shirt. He gritted his teeth. Mia North. No, none of this had her name on it, but he knew it. She'd been at this commune. No, he didn't have fingerprints or solid evidence. It gave him that itch in the back of his head, whenever he was on to something.

But he'd missed her.

As usual.

Once again, he was a step behind. Like always.

But he was getting closer. No way would he give up, now.

Letting the cold air slam against his overheated face, he looked out into the desert. Mexico. It was just over that ridge. And there were no fences, in this remote section of Texas. The Border Patrol might've stopped people from trying to come into this country, but they wouldn't care much about someone leaving it.

So had she? Had she crossed the border into Mexico? Was she sitting on a beach, looking out at the clear blue water, maybe drinking a tropical cocktail?

He smiled at the thought.

Hell, no.

A lot of criminals would say that was the dream. But that wasn't Mia North. No, he'd been chasing her long enough to know that wasn't who she was. If she had been looking for a free and easy escape to the islands, she would've done it already. She wouldn't have meandered about the area, dodging in and out of the shadows, solving cases on her way.

No, she wanted something. Something she could only get here.

Justice.

Whatever it was, he knew exactly where she'd go after this.

So right now, his only aim was to get back to Dallas.

He pulled out onto the highway, headed North. As he was drumming his fingers on the steering wheel, listening to "Sweet Home Alabama" on the radio, his phone began to ring.

It was Dana, his wife.

He turned down the radio and pressed the button on his dashboard. "Hi, Dearest."

"I'll have you know you didn't call me yet, today," she said. She sounded stern but after over thirty years of marriage, he knew when she was teasing him.

"I was just about to."

"Right. Sure you were." She snorted.

"How are things going there?" he asked her. Right now, he could just picture her, in the garden of their house outside of Corpus Christi, where they'd lived their entire married lives. Even though they'd technically put down roots there, his job had him away from home most of the year. Dana was very good at being single, though—they might not have had children, but she had her hobbies, her friends, her social engagements, her dinners out.

"Oh, it's going. Though that rose bush you planted last month is about dead. I think the beetles got to it."

"Damn. That's too bad," he said, with a pang of homesickness. He'd liked that day, working in the garden with her, between jobs. The smell of the roses, the dirt under his fingernails, the lemonade she'd made him after a long, hard day. It'd only been a month ago, and yet it felt like years since he'd seen her face.

"It's all right. But I think I'm giving up on it. Tonight's mahjong night, so I'm going to have to get ready for that."

He nodded. Every week, for the last twenty years, she and a group of her friends had gotten together to play. "I'm sure you'll have fun."

"Oh, I know I will," she said, and he could hear the smile in her voice. "The only way it would be funner is if you were here, too."

He smiled. "Funner isn't a word. You'd think a former first grade teacher would know that."

“I just do it because I know it gets your panties in a bunch,” she said with a laugh. “Call me later.”

“I will, Dearest,” he said, and disconnected the call. The second it ended, the loneliness hit him, hard. It always did, and he had to power through it by thinking about what he’d do the next time he saw Dana in person. Now, he imagined them, working together, taking that rose bush out, maybe planting some tomatoes . . .

It was in the midst of those thoughts that it hit him.

There was another thing Mia North could only get in one place. Her family.

Her husband wasn’t talking. No one in her family really had. But he knew exactly who would.

He’d been keeping tabs on the older sister, Francine Clopecki. She was a police officer, too. And it’d only taken a couple calls to her precinct to learn that she’d taken a couple days off “for personal reasons.” A little more digging around, and he’d found out that she’d rented a hotel room outside of Del Rio, on the Mexican border.

He doubted that was for a little vacation. A lot of her activity had been suspicious.

So Kane Wilcox knew exactly who he should talk to.

*

Kane Wilcox made the 400-mile trip back to Dallas in record time. When he arrived at the address for Mia North’s sister, a small condo development near Morris Lake, it was about dinnertime.

He knocked on the door, and there was no answer. As he was about to leave, wondering if he needed to track her down at the precinct, he heard something crash inside. He knocked again. “Francine Clopecki? Are you in there?”

The door opened slightly, and a single blue eye, covered in mascara, regarded him. “Who are you?”

He showed his badge. “Agent Wilcox from the U.S. Marshals. I have some questions about your sister?”

“I don’t have answers.”

Yeah, I bet you don’t. “I heard a crash. Is everything all right in there?”

“Yep. Just . . . my cat.” She looked away, behind her. “And I don’t have any answers because I haven’t seen Mia since before she was arrested.”

There was a definite harshness to her tone, as well as a bit of fear. She wouldn't be . . . no, it wasn't possible. Would she be harboring Mia there, now?

He tried to peer behind her, but she closed the door more. "Ms. Clopecki, I have a report that Mia North, your sister, was down in a town called Bracketville."

The woman made no reaction. "And?"

"And I have learned that you also took out a hotel room in Bracketville, a few days ago. You called out of work and—"

"So? I wanted a vacation."

"You didn't see Mia while you were there?"

She shook her head.

"You have no idea where your sister is?"

"Nope. None."

"May I come in?"

"No."

"Why's that?"

She scowled at him. "Because my house is a mess. I wasn't expecting company."

He crossed his arms. "Or are you hiding something?"

The standoff was tense. As he stood there, staring her down, a white blur appeared at his feet, scurrying out the door and down the hallway.

Francine's eyes went wide. "Puffball! Come back!" She threw open the door and rushed after him.

Wilcox took the moment to peer into her apartment. Sure enough, it was messy. But there was no sign of Mia North, that he could see.

"If you think I'm hiding my sister in there, you're crazy," a voice said.

He turned. Standing in front of him was a heavy-set woman with white-blonde hair and a neat uniform. The brass nameplate on her breast said, Clopecki. She was petting the white cat in her arms.

"You can't blame me for being suspicious," he said.

She sighed. "I guess I can't. But I'm telling you, I don't know a thing."

He leaned against the jamb. "How about this? You tell me what you know, and I'll make sure you don't lose your badge and get thrown in jail for aiding and abetting a wanted criminal?"

Her eyes went wide, but only for a moment. "Look. I'm not an idiot. You need to have evidence that I helped her, and you don't. All you have is a credit card slip? You'll need to do better than that."

"And what if I told you I have witnesses that have seen you two together?" he bluffed.

She smiled. "I'd say, bullshit."

That was the problem with dealing with other people in law enforcement. They knew the law so well, they could find ways to wiggle around it.

"Agent Wilcox," she said carefully, stroking her cat slowly. "You don't know who you're dealing with. She's Mia North. She was a damn fine FBI agent. And she's not going to put any of us in danger by making us aware of where she might be. So when I tell you I have no idea where she is, I'm not lying. I really don't know."

He studied her closely. Damn. She was telling the truth.

She pushed aside the door and said, "Come on in. You can search the place, if you'd like. You won't find anything. Mia's too smart for that."

He stroked his chin. There was no point in that.

"What if I told you I didn't just want to bring Mia in? What if I told you that her story intrigues me, and I want to know more about it?"

She chuckled, low. "I'd say I don't trust you, Marshal. And neither will she." She shrugged. "What is it that you want to know? If she is innocent? Is that the big question?"

"Do you think she is?"

Francine shook her head. "No. It's not a question to me at all. I *know* she is innocent."

He raised an eyebrow. "You do? That's sister's love—"

"No, it's not. I love the law. My whole family does. We have a big respect for it. If she was guilty of what they said she was, I'd say fine, put her in jail. If Mia truly was guilty, she'd have turned herself in. But there are whisperings, things you can't say out loud, unless you want to land yourself in a lot of hot water."

"Whisperings of what?"

She shrugged, as if the answer was obvious. "That Mia was framed for murder by someone very powerful, who wanted her out of the way."

"Someone . . . who?"

Francine smiled. "Aw, Agent. I can't give you all the answers, or I suspect it wouldn't be any fun for you. I think if you looked into it yourself, you might find out. And then you'll be doing us all a favor, because then Mia can finally come home."

Kane Wilcox stared at her. He'd heard and seen some zany things in this line of work, but this was the craziest. This former FBI agent, playing Superwoman and swooping in, solving crimes while on the lam from the supposed good guys. "How about this. You ever get in touch with her again, tell her I'd like to talk to her. Off the record. I want to hear what she knows."

Francine laughed. "I'm not in touch with her, remember? And I'd sooner scale Mount Everest than get her to meet with the likes of you. So nice try."

He turned away and headed back to his car. This was a waste. She was a locked vault and wouldn't tell him anything about her sister, even if she did know it. He'd have to figure out something else, maybe go to the local police and see if they'd noticed any suspicious activity in the area.

Because she was here, and close by. Maybe even in University Park. He could feel it.

CHAPTER SIX

The gauge on Mia's gas tank was on the E by the time she made it to the Econo-Fill, ten miles north of University Park. It was one of the few gas stations she'd never been to before.

It was also only about half a mile away from Lookout Point, where those bodies were found.

She parked in front of the gas pump and let out a big sigh. *Nope, Mia. You're not doing it. You can't get involved. Be strong.*

She nodded, getting comfortable with the decision. After all, the police probably had a grip on it. Two murders of young people, in the prime of their lives? The news had been everywhere. It'd even made national headlines. It was very likely that Linda was wrong and the police were throwing all their manpower at it. They just hadn't told her. It wouldn't be the first time they kept the victims' families in the dark while they continued their investigation. The police would probably announce a suspect shortly.

"Definitely," she whispered to herself, climbing out of the car, into the relentless mid-day heat. Even in the shade of the gas station's overhang, it was at least ninety degrees, and her shirt, which she'd had to wash in the sink of the last hotel room, clung to her with sweat, stiff and drab. She went inside the convenience store, rummaging through her wallet for a couple of twenties.

There were two registers open, side-by-side, in the inside convenience store. She grabbed a pack of gum and laid it in front of the sullen boy behind the counter. "This, and whatever's left, for regular," she said, motioning outside. "Pump eight."

"Got it," the kid said, punching into the register.

As she was waiting, she noticed the headline on the newspaper, *The Dallas Morning News,* in the rack between the two registers: POLICE STILL BAFFLED IN LOOKOUT POINT DOUBLE MURDER.

At the next register over, the pudgy man who was paying for his sandwich tapped the paper. "Not for long," he said with a grin. "Did you hear?"

"What do you mean?" the older lady said, leaning forward with both pale elbows on the counter, so she could see the front page. "Oh, that. That was a terrible story. And too close to home. I live just down from there. In those woods. I could've found those bodies myself if I'd taken my Bruno for a walk that night. We go through that way all the time. I'm scared to go now, because the killer's still out there."

He waved his hand. "That's what I'm saying. I've heard they do know who did it, and it's pretty shocking news."

Mia was hanging on his every word, so much so that she didn't hear the teenage cashier until he snapped his fingers in her face. "Pump eight's ready," he said, shoving the pack of gum over to her.

"Oh, thanks," she said, taking the gum and backing away, still listening to the man at the counter, who was grinning with his precious information, looking like he was trying to draw it out for suspense.

Then he leaned forward and said something in a dramatic whisper, but she couldn't quite hear it, because he was faced away from her. Whatever he said, it made the female cashier's eyes bug out. "Are you kidding me? How selfish! That poor girl. How do you know?"

Mia processed the words, trying to understand what could possibly lead to that kind of reaction. *Selfish? Poor girl? What about the boy, Jason?*

Like a lightning bolt, the answer hit her.

No. Not possible. It couldn't be . . .

"I know because I deliver the mail around there," he said, and for the first time Mia realized he was wearing the postal worker's uniform, dark blue shorts that clung to his thick thighs and a lighter blue shirt, stretched tight over the substantial curve of his back. "And I heard the policemen at the precinct talking about it."

"Excuse me," Mia blurted, making both of them turn. "Did you say something about the murder of those two young people? Kiki Redbone and Jason Sawyer-Delaney?"

The man faced her and nodded. "Yep, I was just saying, it's not a double homicide. The boy was messed up in the head, couldn't take the idea of leaving high school and moving on to college. They think he killed his girlfriend and then turned the gun on himself because he didn't want to live anymore."

So it *was* just as she'd thought. Her mouth opened. At first, nothing came out, but then she murmured, "That can't be right."

The postman shrugged. "They seem to think it's pretty open and shut. I guess they asked around and found out the kid talked to a lot of people about his depression. He was in a mental hospital last year because he took a lot of pills."

Linda's son? Jason? I can't even believe that. Not that smiling boy whose picture was on the wall of her house.

But Mia knew better than anyone that looks could be deceiving. Just look at Wilson Andrews.

Besides, depressed people often didn't scream it out loud for everyone to hear. But even if he had been depressed, would he have murdered his girlfriend before killing himself? *I wonder if he owned the murder weapon. I could've asked Linda that when I talked to her.*

Of course, back then, she'd been adamant that she would not be taking the case. That she would be staying as far as possible away from it.

And now, here she was, with questions upon questions, building up inside her.

And Lookout Point was just a little bit down the road.

"Ma'am," the cashier said. "You gonna get your gas or what?"

She nodded slowly, then looked around and realized both cashiers and the postman were staring at her curiously. If she didn't want to make a scene, this probably wasn't the way to go about it.

"Yeah, thanks so much," she said, shoving the pack of gum into her pocket and heading outside to pump her gas.

After that, she'd take an innocent little walk through the woods.

*

Mia had never actually been to Lookout Point after dark.

Oh, she'd been there before, during the day, as a child, because the fields surrounding the place were a popular place for picnics. It was lovely, with plenty of wooden tables, overlooking the city. As she drove down the dirt road to the parking lot, she thought of the times she'd come here with her family, when Francine used to chase her around the woods. Then she'd make kissing noises and hug herself, pretending to make out with her boyfriend.

Of course, Francine had *plenty* of boyfriends, as a young woman, and had probably come here *many* times. But Mia had been the late bloomer who usually stayed home, in her bedroom on Saturday nights, alone.

Before she reached the clearing of the parking lot, Mia made a turn and parked off to the side, on a shoulder choked with pine needles and poison ivy. She stepped out of the car and walked through the woods, looking for the yellow crime scene tape. She found it, blocking the entrance to the lot, with a sign that said, *Area Closed.* There was a single police car parked in the lot.

Keeping low, she navigated the perimeter of the lot, using the cover of trees to stay out of sight. She didn't see the officer at first, but as she made her way to the back of the lot, she heard his footsteps crunching on dead leaves in the woods. Ducking down behind a bush, she watched him walk back to his car, get inside, and head out, pausing only to remove the tape and re-set it once he'd gone through the barrier.

She let out a breath of relief. Alone.

She turned and headed in the direction she'd seen the officer come from. Sure enough, as she got closer, she found the yellow crime scene tape, forming a lopsided rectangle around the perimeter, about the size of one of the many No-Tell Motel rooms she'd stayed at, since she'd gone on the run. Ducking underneath the tape, she slowly walked to the center of it, keeping her eyes peeled to the ground.

It was muddy, and there were a lot of footprints to be found. The prints looked like they'd come mostly from smooth bottoms—the standard Dallas police uniform shoes. But there were others, half-buried. Smaller feet, sneakers, with the tell-tale marking of Vans. Other than that, not much. The police had likely combed the place over. She walked along, trying not to make her own footprints in the now-dry mud, looking for anything they might have missed, but the footprints were the only trace.

She squatted to look more closely at them when a deep male voice said, "Hey."

The officer came back. That was her first thought. Jumping up, Mia almost broke into a run. But then she noticed a man with a thick beard and trucker's hat, wearing a flannel shirt and carrying a rifle, standing behind the tape. A hunter? Well, this was Texas, after all.

"Hey," she said carefully.

"You know you're not supposed to be there," the man said, looking back toward the parking lot. "That's what this here tape is for."

She nodded. "Yeah, I—"

"Couple kids' bodies were found right in that spot." He shook his head. "Damn shame."

"I heard."

His eyes narrowed. "What are you, one of those internet celebrities? Taking video to show to your followers?"

"No." She held up her hands to show she didn't have a phone to take pictures. "I'm . . . I'm just a friend of the boy's mother."

"Ah," he said, ducking under the tape and coming closer to her. "Sorry about that kid. I've been hunting in these woods all my life and never heard nothing like that. It makes this place different somehow. Eerie. I don't know if I want to keep hunting here anymore."

"These are hunting grounds?" she said, looking at his gun.

He smirked. "Yeah, but don't get any ideas. The kids weren't killed with a hunting rifle. It was a handgun."

"How do you know that?"

He shrugged. "I might've been around when the bodies were found. Young girl who found the bodies was screaming bloody murder, so I stayed with her to make sure she was okay. So I was here when the police showed up. They questioned me. I heard some things."

"You did?"

"Yep." He took in a deep breath and let it out as he stared out over the Dallas skyline. He clearly wasn't in the rush to tell it that Mia was in to hear it. "Both shot in the head with a single bullet, same caliber. They weren't dumped there. They were killed right where they were found. Why they were there? Maybe just came out to enjoy Lookout Point, like all kids do. Stands to reason."

The words the postman had said rang heavily in her ears. They hadn't sat right, ever since she heard them. "Do you know if the weapon was found there? I heard the police think it's a case of murder-suicide, that the boy killed the girl, and then himself."

He shrugged. "I don't know about any weapon, but as for murder-suicide, I don't believe that."

"Why?"

"Because I was one of the first people on the scene."

"And?"

"Tracking runs in my family. I learned it from my daddy, who learned it from his. We've been hunting these grounds forever. Usually animals, but I notice other things, too." He motioned her forward, then pointed to the ground. "All these flat footprints are police, right?"

She nodded. "I thought so."

"And these small sneaker prints here belong to the girl who found the couple—you see?"

She followed closely behind him. "Yes. I agree."

Then he came to a spot where the earth had been disturbed. “Round here is exactly where the bodies were found. The boy here.” He pointed, then pointed to another spot. “The girl here.”

“All right.”

“I can make out traces of their footprints, here and . . .” He took a large step and pointed. “There. They might’ve started out at Lookout Point, but they might’ve taken a roundabout route, because from the direction their shoes are pointed, they were returning to the Point, going in the opposite direction. You got that?”

“Yes, but . . . where were they coming from?”

He shrugged. “Don’t know, but here’s the interesting thing.” He hooked a finger at her.

She followed him, but before he could speak, she noticed it. She bent over the footprint from a rugged-soled work boot, to look closer. “Whose are those?”

He shrugged. “Don’t know. But I know they ain’t new, from some looky-loo like you who’s got that morbid fascination to hang around crime scenes. I saw them that night. What I don’t understand is--”

“Is why the police would think it’s a murder-suicide if they have the footprints of another person at the scene,” she interrupted, breathing the words almost to herself.

“Bingo,” he said, a bright smile peeking out of his bushy beard. “It’s a mystery, ain’t it?”

“Thank you,” she said, heading the way she’d come and ducking under the tape. She couldn’t just let this go. She needed to make sure the police knew that Jason Delaney-Sawyer wasn’t a murderer. Somehow.

CHAPTER SEVEN

It wasn't hard to find Linda Delaney-Sawyer's phone number. Mia hadn't noticed it before, but it turned out that Linda was now a real estate agent, and so her name and likeness was splashed on billboards and signs all over town.

What *was* hard was finding a payphone that still worked. In the past month, she'd been using and dumping burner phones like crazy, but she thought for this call, she'd just use a payphone. No such luck, she realized, as she drove through a shopping center, finding no public phones.

There was, however, a small electronics store. She went inside, bought the cheapest model she could find, and dialed the number on the giant *SELL YOUR HOME FAST WITH LINDA BY YOUR SIDE!* billboard across the highway.

"This is Linda," a voice said in monotone.

"Hi, Linda. This is—"

"Yeah, I'm sorry to tell you but I'm not working for the next few weeks due to a personal matter. If you'd like, I can give you the names of other agents—"

"Oh, no. Linda. This is Mia. Mia North. I just left your house a couple hours ago."

"Oh! Mia." There was a confused pause. "Why are you calling me on my work line? You have my regular number, don't you?"

"Sorry, I have a . . . new phone, and all of my regular numbers are gone," she said, which wasn't a lie. "But—"

"I hate it when that happens. Well, let me give it to you, so you have it. We really should get the girls together for a sleepover."

Linda recited it, and Mia scribbled it down. "Thanks," she said quickly. "But I wanted to ask you, have the police told you anything about the murder weapon?"

"The murder weapon? No. Other than that it was a gun."

"Did Jason have a gun?"

"Yes. Well, a hunting rifle."

"But no handgun?"

"No, of course not. He only went hunting with his father a couple of weekends every year. The gun's still under lock and key in the basement, too. I'm sure of it."

"Did the family have any other guns?"

"Just two hunting rifles. That's all." There was a pause. "Why are you asking? I thought you said--"

"I might be reconsidering," she said, gnawing on her lip.

"Oh, really, how great, you have no idea how glad I am to—"

"Linda, it's very important that no one knows I'm on this case. Do you understand? I'm supposed to be elsewhere, and if my supervisors find out—"

"Oh, yes. I understand. Your secret is safe with me."

"Good. So, did Jason have issues with his mental health?"

Another pause. "Yes, he did. His sophomore year in high school, he went through a rough patch. But he made it through. And he was fine."

"A rough patch? What does that mean?"

"He was suicidal. Spent a few days in a hospital upstate. But when he came back, he was on meds, and seeing a therapist regularly. That really helped. His junior year, he got out of it. And he was doing well. We were so proud of him, because his grades had really dipped his sophomore year, but he worked to get them up, get accepted at UT Dallas."

"And how was he, the last time you saw him? Was he nervous or acting strange?"

"Not at all. He was excited. He couldn't wait to graduate and move on to the next chapter," she said, her voice cracking.

Which means that the police's theory is total BS, Mia thought. She didn't want to upset Linda any further by telling her what the postman had said. After all, it was still just a rumor.

"What are you thinking?" Linda prompted, when she hadn't spoken in a few seconds.

"I went to the crime scene. I looked around. There wasn't much there, but I did see footprints that concern me. I have a few things I'd like to look into. But what I'd really appreciate is the names of some of their mutual friends, people the two were close with. Do you have that?" she asked.

"Well, I do. I'm sure his phone would have all that information, but the police took that."

"Yes, unfortunately, since I'm not FBI anymore, I don't have a way of looking into that," Mia said, though she wished she could. If she were David, or Francine, all of this would be so much easier. But she couldn't even contact them. Not now. It was too dangerous.

"Okay, well, let's see. Jason's wingman, he called him—his best friend— has always been River Alvarez. He always used to joke that River was the third wheel in their relationship. And Kiki's best friend was Tori Schloss. I think they double-dated a few times recently."

Mia scribbled this down and checked the dashboard. It was almost two-thirty, which meant that high schools would soon be letting out. "They went to . . . Park High?"

"Oak Cliff High," she said.

That was familiar to Mia. She'd been there recently, to investigate murders involving some high school students. But that wasn't necessarily a good thing—she didn't want to be seen in the same place twice, even if she'd last been there three weeks ago. It wasn't smart.

But it wouldn't hurt to just check it out.

"If you want to talk to them, though, you should probably go to the place, where they work," she said. "They're all senior year early release, so I bet they're at the ice cream shop."

"Oh." Good news. "What ice cream shop?"

"Sundae School, in Oak Cliff."

"Thanks. Perfect," she said, capping her pen. "I'm going to check it out and ask them a few questions."

She let out a sigh of relief. "Thanks, Mia. And if I think of anyone else you should talk to, I'll let you know. Can I text you at this number?"

"Absolutely," Mia said. *Until I have to dump it for the next phone.*

*

Sundae School was an old building from the 1950s, sock-hop days, with a sign shaped like a giant vanilla ice cream cone with sprinkles. There was even a giant cherry on top. The place had been around even when Mia was a child, under a different name, though she'd only gone there once because there were other ice cream shops closer to where she grew up.

Mia pulled a hat and sunglasses on for disguise, and got out of her car, glad to see there was only a mother with her two kids at the picnic benches in front, and no line at the window. When she approached, a girl with a blonde ponytail said, with little emotion, "Welcome to Sundae School, can I interest you in our famous double-dipper?"

Mia took a chance. "Are you Tori Schloss?"

The girl rolled her eyes. "Oh, God, what now? Are you police?"

"Yes," Mia lied, hoping she wouldn't ask for a badge. "I just have a few more questions to clear up, for you and . . ." She scrambled to open the crumpled piece of paper and read the name.

"River," she muttered, then looked around the back and shouted, "River. Fuzz is here to talk to us again."

"Do you mind?"

She checked her phone, then started to pull off her paper hat and apron. "No. As long as it doesn't take too long, I guess I can take my break."

She looked over at an older, Hispanic woman who nodded. "Go," the woman said, glaring at Mia, "But they must be back for the afterschool rush."

"No problem," Mia said, navigating to the picnic benches. She went to one of the few tables that offered the shade of an umbrella. By then, the mother and kids had already taken off. She sat at a bench, and a few moments later, the couple arrived. The girl was wearing a summery flowered dress and flip flops, her ears pierced dozens of times, sipping from a vanilla shake. She was a full foot shorter than the boy, who was wearing shorts, tall sport socks, and a Dallas Cowboys jersey, his dark hair clipped close to his head.

He narrowed his eyes at her as he straddled the bench across from her. "You're a cop?"

"Yes," Mia said dismissively. "I just had a few more questions to clear up about the death of your friends. You four were all close?"

River nodded. "I've known Jason since we were in kindergarten."

"I've known Kiki just about as long," Tori offered. "And when they started dating, we did, too. But it's not like we were a love match. We were just together out of convenience. They were in love."

She eyed River with a bit of disgust, and his look in response was of one of obvious dejection. Mia got the feeling that River didn't share her sentiment and wanted it to be a love match. But he simply looked down at his hands, not speaking.

"When was the last time you saw them?"

Tori looked into her shake and started to stir it. "In school that afternoon. I wanted to go shopping with Kiki, but she and Jason had other plans. They were going to the carnival."

"And you didn't want to go with them?"

"Nope. They knew better than to ask me to that carnival. I used to work there every year and I hate it."

River shrugged. "They didn't ask me at all. I had a baseball game that night. So I told Jason I'd catch him later that weekend. I texted him a couple times, and no response. Odd, but I figured he was just busy. I didn't hear until Sunday morning what had happened."

Tori nodded. "Me neither."

"The carnival was . . ."

"The Fire Department Carnival. They have it at the fairgrounds every year. That's why they were up there," she said.

"There was a carnival there? By Lookout Point?" Mia asked.

The kids nodded.

That made sense. Beyond the woods, there was a large expanse of open land, leading toward the city, and it had been scattered with refuse. But that meant that if they'd gone to the carnival, they might have met up with some drifters who wanted their money and killed them for it. She'd have to look into that later. "So they weren't at Lookout Point?"

River's eyes narrowed. "They were probably going there. But they were at the carnival. Um, you should know that, because that's where his car was found. In the carnival parking lot."

"Right," Mia said, looking down at her phone. "I just have a lot of notes here. Do you happen to know if either of them had enemies? Were they into anything like drugs, gangs, that sort of thing?"

Tori laughed. "Drugs? Gangs? Them? No, they were squeaky clean. Which is why this was all so shocking. I'm surprised my mom let me leave the house to come to work, she's so worried."

"So you think it's just random? You don't think there's anyone that Kiki or Jason knew who might have—"

"If there's anyone, it's Brick." She and River exchanged a nervous glance.

"Brick? Is that a person?"

Tori nodded. "His name is Bronson Shu, but everyone on the football team calls him Brick. He's built like a wall, you know, a brick wall." She shrugged. "Kiki dated him before Jason. It was pretty serious because it went on her whole sophomore year. But when she broke it off, he went crazy. Started sending all these threatening texts."

Which I should know about, since the "police" confiscated her phone. "Right, yes. I think I read about that in the report. You think this kid might've escalated things?"

River nodded. "He made threats all the time. He even said once that he was going to kill her. That was at a football game. Everyone heard."

"When was that?"

"Last fall. Few months ago."

She made a note on her phone: *Bronson Shu.* "And where do you think he might be now?"

They looked at each other. "Gym."

Mia's stomach lurched. The last thing she wanted to do was go back there. "The Oak Cliff High School Gym?"

"No," River said. "Vinnie's Gym, on Post Road? That's where the athletes go. It's like, old-school, pump-you-up gym. Not the kind with fruity exercise classes and juice bars."

"Oh, gotcha." She made a note of that, too, and as she was about to ask another question, she heard a woman, clearing her voice, behind her.

She turned to find the kids' manager, glaring at them and motioning to a couple new cars that had parked in the lot. Sure enough, families with kids were heading for the line.

The teens sprang up. Tori said, "If you don't need us anymore . . ."

"No, I'm good. Thanks," she said, waving at them as they hurried back to deal with the after-school rush.

She sat there for a moment, under shade of the umbrella, staring at the notes she'd taken on her phone. It was time to pay a visit to this Brick Shu.

CHAPTER EIGHT

The hot, dank air smelled of sweat and testosterone as Mia stepped into the gym. River had been right. The long, narrow room was only for the serious weightlifter. There wasn't a cardio machine in sight. There were various machines and free weights scattered over dusty mats, and the walls were covered with mirrors. The sound of several beefy men grunting and weights clanking echoed through the giant room.

"You're not here to lift," the older woman behind the front counter noted, studying her from head to toe. "Let me guess. You want to buy a gift for your honey?"

She pointed to a display case, showing various items such as Vinnie's tank tops, koozies, and lifting gloves. But Mia shook her head. "No, actually, I'm looking for someone. Bronson Shu?"

She grinned. "You mean Brick?"

Mia nodded. "Yes, right. Can I talk to him?"

"You could if he were here. He left, maybe ten minutes ago," she said with a shrug. "You just missed him. "

"I did?" She frowned and looked out to the parking lot. "Did he happen to say where he was going?"

"Hey, Moose!" The woman screamed across the room, so loud that Mia's eardrums shook.

A large, dark-skinned man with tree-trunks for legs and bulging muscles on his chest, dropped his weight at the Smith Machine and came sauntering over, giving Mia an eye-raking. "What's so important you needed to interrupt my leg work out?"

"You were talking to Brick, earlier. Did you hear where he was going?"

He nodded. "Wally's. Said he was getting drunk."

Wally's. She knew the place. It was a dive, biker bar she used to drive past every day on her way to work. But she never thought about going in. Never wanted to. It was a place for tough people, the kind without any windows, which made you wonder what kind of illegal things were going on inside. What was a teenage kid doing, going in there? "Are you sure you've got the right kid? He can't even be eighteen; he's a high school kid."

"Whoops," Moose said, shrugging his massive shoulders. "What are you, his truant officer or something? He told me he had a fake ID. Are you gonna get him in trouble?"

"No," she said. "I just want to talk to him. He comes here a lot, does he?"

The man chuckled and sauntered back to the machines. "Ol' Brick's here more than the owners, right, Charlie?"

The woman at the counter nodded. "Brick's here all the time. Every member here has a key, so they can come in twenty-four-seven."

"Do you have a record of when people come here?"

She nodded and pulled out a log book. "We make people sign this book when they come in. They don't always do it, but they're supposed to. And we have cameras, so if they don't, we give 'em a slap on the wrist. Brick's pretty good about it, though."

Mia opened the book and scanned it. Sure enough, there were a lot of entries for a Brick Shu. He was clearly their most ardent member. She scanned down to the date for last Friday night. Sure enough, his name was there. He'd been there from eight until eleven at night.

But that didn't mean it was true. He could've written that there, hoping to use it as his alibi. "You have video?"

She nodded. "All the time."

"Can I see it?"

"I guess. It'll take some time to . . . wait." The woman closed the book quickly and eyed her with suspicion. "What are you? A cop? I'm not going to show the video to just anyone off the street."

She shook her head. "Forget it. But you check the video, right? So if someone went against the rules, you'd know?"

"Yep, every morning, and then we issue a warning if someone doesn't follow the rules," she said, sounding annoyed, her hands on her hips. "Anything else?"

"No, thank you."

She stepped outside, gnawing on her lip. Brick might have had an alibi, or maybe not. Maybe those people were covering for him? Either way, Brick Shu was her only lead, and he might have information.

Like it or not, it was time to stop by the dive bar, Wally's.

*

Wally's hadn't changed for the better since the last time she'd seen it. In fact, it looked even scarier. There were a dozen motorcycles parked out front, even more dented old pick-up trucks in the lot, and the only windows were covered in frosted cubes, with Michelob and Miller Light neon signs in them. A sign outside, missing quite a few letters, proclaimed, *Wal y's Wag n Wheel – Hap y H ur T days 4-6.*

Bracing herself, Mia pulled her collar up around her face and walked in the front door.

Immediately, she was engulfed in smoke, pretty funny, considering smoking was illegal indoors, even in Texas. Apparently, they hadn't gotten the memo here. She heard the honky-tonk music playing on the jukebox, saw the pool tables through the haze of smoke, and stepped inside, hating every moment of it.

The men in there, some dressed in leather vests, others in denim, plaid, and cowboy hats, glared at her. She forced a smile as she made her way to the nose-ringed bartender, who was busy pouring three shots of Jack. "What can I get you?" he said in a gruff voice,

"I'm looking for Brick Shu," she said, lowering her voice to try to sound more intimidating. "Do you know him?"

"Who's asking? Police?"

She knew better than to say she was police among this gang. They'd probably never let her see the light of day again. "His mother," she said. "He needs to come home to dinner."

The man raised an eyebrow, then an amused grin appeared among his whiskers. Around her, other men started to laugh, and one of them shouted, "Bricky! Your mommy's here to fetch you!"

All attention seemed to turn toward the pool tables. The bartender motioned her that way. "There in the corner."

There were a lot of people packed into the corner, and the smoke was thick, but she didn't need to look twice. She spotted Brick Shu immediately, sitting on a stood, holding a pool cue and glaring at her. He was a big Asian man, about as wide as two men put together, dwarfing the little stool under his backside. He had a wide forehead, made bigger because his black hair was pulled back harshly into a ponytail at the back of his skull.

"What the hell do you want?" he growled as she approached and stood at the other end of the pool table.

Around her, people seemed to stop their conversations and turn to look at them. She took in a deep breath and let it out, trying to calm herself. "Brick Shu? Can we go someplace quiet and talk?"

He looked around, pulled the mug of beer from a nearby table, and chugged it. “Hell no.” He motioned to the pool table. “I’m winning this game.”

She moved closer, hoping the rest of the bar would go back to minding their own business. “Fine. I’ll wait until you’re done.”

“How about you screw off?” he said, chugging his beer.

She crossed her arms. “How about you just come with me, and your mom won’t kick your ass?”

He choked, spewing beer everywhere. A loud roar of laughter erupted around them. Mia felt a surge of adrenaline thrum through her veins, followed quickly by a pang of regret. *If you don’t want to call attention to yourself, Mia, this isn’t the way to go about it.*

“Go with your mommy, Shu!” a burly man said behind her, to more laughter. “You need to have your diaper changed!”

He wiped his mouth and set the stick and the beer down. “Fine. But you owe me twenty dollars,” he mumbled, sounding every bit of the teenager he was, despite his massive size.

Head down, he followed her out to the front of the building. When they were standing there among the motorcycles, he said, sounding nothing like the jerk she’d met inside, “You a friend of my mom’s? Is she all right?”

Mia had been staring at his shoes. They weren’t work boots, like the footprints she’d seen in the field, and for such a big guy, he had rather petite feet. He was wearing white sneakers. She shook her head distractedly when she realized he’d asked her a question. “I’m sorry. Your mother? What do you mean?”

“My mom. You know her, right? She asked you to come get me?”

Suddenly, she understood. He was talking about the excuse she’d given to speak to him. “No, I just said that to get you to come out here. This is about Kiki Redbone—”

“What?” he spun to face her, his eyes blazing. “So this isn’t about my mom?”

“No, it’s—”

“Hell!” He scrubbed his hands down his face. “I thought she was in trouble. She’s always getting in trouble, working our store downtown. She’s been robbed three times this year.”

“Oh. No. I don’t know your mom,” she said.

“Okay. Then what the hell was that all about? You better have a good reason for pulling me out of there.” His face twisted to a scowl. “Wait. Did you say this was about Kiki?”

She nodded. “I hear you dated her.”

“I did. Long time ago. But I have nothing good to say about her. Far as I’m concerned, she was a bitch. And I’m glad she’s dead.”

Mia raised an eyebrow. That was harsh. “And her boyfriend?”

“Jason? Kid’s a little prick. Have no idea what she saw in him.” He leaned against the railing and stared up at the darkened sky. “If you ask me, they got what they deserved.”

Mia stared at him. “Oh. Is that right?”

He nodded, but seemed to realize what he was saying because he lowered his head and shook it. “Look, I don’t know who you are, if you’re police or whatever, but if you’re thinking I killed them, you’re wrong. I don’t care enough about either of them to risk my future like that.”

“You sent her threatening messages, even just recently. And you told her you were going to kill her.”

His eyes narrowed. “How did you . . . so what? I said some things, yeah. Texted some things, too. Usually while I was drunk, so I couldn’t even tell you what I said.” He shrugged. “I didn’t mean anything. I swear on it. I’m going to West Point in the fall. I got accepted. Why would I care about them when I have that?”

Mia shrugged. “Maybe because you loved her? And jealousy makes people do crazy things?”

He shook his head. “No. I didn’t. Not that much, anyway. I know we were wrong for each other. I saw her with that prick, and she was always so much happier than she was with me. So I guess they were made for each other.” He scrubbed his hands down his face. “Look, I don’t know who you are, but listen. I heard they were killed on Friday night, right? Well, I was in the gym. You can check with them.”

“I just came from there. And yes, you were in the gym from eight until eleven. But there’s nothing saying you couldn’t have killed them later that night.”

His lips twisted. “I guess not. But I didn’t. I did bis and tris that night. After a workout that long, I usually go right home and crash.” He started to play with a seam on the edge of his tank-top. “You could ask my mom, but she doesn’t speak much English.”

Mia shook her head. “It’s all right. But can you tell me . . . you probably don’t know Kiki very well anymore, or Jason, for that matter. Do you have any idea who might’ve killed them?”

“Yep. Kiki was like that. Cheerleader type. Had lots of guys swarming around her. And she was a tease. Always loved the attention.

I bet one of them went after her." He smiled. "So you had the right idea, with me. Only I'm the wrong guy."

"Can you name some of those guys that you might have seen her with? Ones that might have gotten the wrong idea and taken it too far."

He started to list them on his fingers. "Josh Hartley. Mick Balboa. Pretty much all of the football team . . ."

She made mental notes of the names, though she got the feeling his was just listing names off the top of his head. "What makes you think that?"

"Kiki was a hot piece. Everyone wanted her."

"But no one ever made threats to her, or him? You never saw this with your own eyes?"

"Nope. But I know people were jealous of her, and I think she probably just pissed off the wrong guy. That's all. Someone from school. Or maybe not."

"Great," she said, walking toward her car.

That was very helpful. She'd keep him on her radar, but it was looking like Brick Shu probably wasn't the right guy.

"Hey . . ." he called after her. "Who the hell are you?"

She didn't turn back. She'd overstayed her welcome here, even though it hadn't been much of a welcome. What she needed to do now was find a place to rest for the night . . . someplace safe from all the people who were looking for her.

CHAPTER NINE

David Hunter sat in the parking lot of the FBI's Dallas Field Office, watching Emmie Valencia make her way to her car.

Emmie Valencia was the receptionist, and clearly, a woman without a life. Though she'd long since passed retirement age, she still came in every day, like clockwork, and stayed for at least twelve hours. The woman was a machine.

She also knew everyone's comings and goings, which was why David had to wait for her to leave before he could go inside. Pembroke had put him on leave, and that's where he needed to stay—away from the office.

And yet, he couldn't. Pembroke's car wasn't in the lot, and in fact, there were only a few remaining cars. As he watched Emmie navigate to the exit in her giant Buick, he decided this was his chance.

He quickly jumped out of his car and ran to the door, grabbing his key card from his pocket. Pembroke would know he'd come into the office . . . tomorrow. But he was going with the "Better to beg for forgiveness than ask permission" motto. If they called him on it, he'd say he forgot his cell phone or something. No problem.

He hoped.

The office was white walls and glass everything, and floors that echoed as he stepped on them, even with his rubber-soled shoes. He walked to the main staircase, a modern, floating series of switchbacks in the center of the three-story foyer, behind the empty reception desk. Quickly climbing the staircase, he stopped at the second floor and moved quickly and quietly as possible to his office.

The lights on the floor weren't out, and there was soft music playing, but no other sound. There was likely a skeleton crew here, as the place never officially closed, but most of the department had called it a night. He made it to his office without seeing a single soul.

Sitting down behind his desk, he turned on his computer, thinking of Mia. It seemed like ages since she'd last been in this office. Her arrest, the trial, all of it was months ago, and yet he'd thought about it every day. He'd been called to take the stand, and he'd said something about her. About her being rash, sometimes acting without thinking. He'd mentioned how pissed Mia had been about Ellis Horvath, stalking her daughter. At the time, he'd thought he was doing the right thing, telling the truth and nothing but the truth.

Now, though, he regretted it, more than anything in his life. Turned out, there was more to it than his perception. A lot more.

Of course, she'd want to protect Kelsey. He'd have been just as angry, had someone been stalking his son Louie. Of course she'd *say* things about wanting him dead. David would've said the same. But saying did not equal doing.

And now, he knew that Mia was innocent. He was a hundred percent sure of that. And the more he'd looked into it, the more he felt like she was on to something when she said that Andrews had set her up, to get her out of the way so that his serial killer brother Jerry could go free and continue to terrorize young girls.

The only thing was, he had no way to convince anyone. No solid evidence. He was just a lowly agent, a cog in the wheel, expected to work on other cases. He'd tried to help her, get her the info that she needed, and it'd landed him on temporary leave.

So he'd have to look into her case, without her help, on his own time, and hope it didn't raise too many eyebrows.

It would, of course. They were watching him now. Like hawks. They'd likely think he was still working with her.

But he couldn't let this go.

At least, now, he could say with absolute conviction that he had no idea where Mia was. It was better that way. For both of them. He'd look into this one thing, for her, leave the info at their drop-off point, hope it would help her case along, and be done with it.

When he logged in, he went to the database and looked up all the past cases that Kevin Reynolds had worked on. The man had been with the Dallas Police for a long time, and that meant thousands of records. But the cases Mia was looking for, she said, involved a young girl. And it had to have happened recently, likely within the year before Mia had been arrested.

To narrow it down, he typed in date limits, and the keywords: *female, youth, adolescent, teenager.*

He scrolled through a number of domestic abuse cases where a child was injured and the assailant was a parent or family member. Several where a child was kidnapped and a perpetrator was caught. Then he came upon a cold case.

He clicked on it, shifting forward in his chair. According to this report, a staff member of an upscale hotel downtown had called the police, concerned after seeing an older man with a girl who appeared to be underage. Reynolds had arrived and interviewed the people staying at the room, and found no evidence of wrongdoing.

The report was notably bare, with very few details. No names of the people interviewed were given. Only the name of the girl. Lila Watkins.

Now, why does that name sound familiar? he thought, navigating to Google. He entered the name in the search bar and turned up thousands of news stories.

The first headline made his skin crawl: *Few Clues in Case of Missing Teen Lila Watkins, Who Disappeared a Year Ago, Today.*

He stared at it until the words blurred together. A year gone. The poor girl was probably dead, the victim of . . .

What? A sinking feeling swirled inside him as the idea took root.

Then he checked the dates, confirming his suspicions.

Kevin Reynolds was called to that upscale hotel where Lila Watkins had been staying, only a week before her disappearance.

But who had she been with? Had she accompanied Wilson Andrews? Or Jerry Andrews, his psycho brother with a penchant for kidnapping young girls? Did it have anything to do with the Andrews brothers at all?

He navigated to the photograph of the girl, in a lavender dress with puff sleeves, taken only a year before her disappearance. She was a pretty girl with pigtails, so young. For her to have been at that hotel, raising eyebrows . . . he had to wonder what they'd seen.

David went back to the report. How stupid. There weren't any names of witnesses interviewed, either. Not even the name of the person who'd called it in.

Either it was shoddy police-work, or a cover up.

But if he remembered what Mia had said, the hitman had told her that Kevin had said he'd regretted not doing more. He dug in his pocket, pulling out the paper she'd left for him, before: *He said something about a girl. How he should've come forward back then, when he first found out about it. He kept saying that, over and over again, how he regretted it . . .*

Pieces were starting to fit together. Maybe Kevin Reynolds regretted not stepping in to do anything for Lila Watkins. And now, she was missing. Possibly dead.

David fumbled around in his desk drawer, trying to find a pen. Quickly, he wrote down the name and some other details of the case on the back of the crumpled, lined sheet of paper. He wasn't sure what or if it had anything to do with the corrupt politician that had put Mia in jail . . . but it was something. A lead.

And one he was sure Mia would want to follow to the end.

Packing up his things, he turned off his computer and made his way out the door, again seeing no one. He'd have to get to the drop-off point tonight, and deliver the goods to Mia. This time, he hoped she'd be able to make something more of it and finally find the information she needed to get home.

CHAPTER TEN

The farther Mia drove out of town, the more unsettled she became.

It should've been the opposite. Out here, in the wide-open Texas landscape, there were fewer people. Fewer police cars patrolling. Fewer chances that she'd stumble upon someone who'd recognize her and bring the Texas State Legal System crashing in on her.

But as she drove away from University Park, she tapped nervously on the steering wheel. She had so much she wanted to look into. She wanted to talk to Linda and find some of the kids' favorite haunts. She wanted to look around the school. She wanted to check into the other people Brick Shu had mentioned. There were so many avenues she could take.

But only if she stayed here in University Park.

Which was, unfortunately, impossible.

And it wasn't just the murder of those kids that kept her wanting to stay close to town. She had her own case to look into, also. All of that was around Dallas, too. She itched to go to the drop-off spot where she'd gotten the information from David, earlier. She wanted to see if he'd had any luck. But she'd only been there the night before. She couldn't keep coming around there. She had to give him time, play it cool.

So her heart grew heavier and heavier as she drove, this time to a little town called Brimley, about forty-five minutes west of the city proper. She found a seedy No-Tell Motel, just like she was used to, called the Horizon Inn. Pulling her hood up to disguise her hair slightly, she went in and got herself a key for the last room on the top floor of the two-story building with sun-faded orange doors.

Trudging to the door, she opened it and inhaled the dank air. All of these motels smelled different . . . but never like anything good. This one, at least, smelled like pine cleaner, giving the impression that it might have been cleaned recently, which was probably a good thing.

She stepped inside and fumbled for a light switch. When she found it, she flipped it on, casting a mediocre, dim orange light over the room. She threw her backpack down on an ugly, palm-tree print comforter, then looked around. Maybe the beach scenes on the walls were supposed to be cheery, but they just made her sad.

She'd been to the beach, once, with Kelsey when she was four or five. South Padre Island. She thought of her little girl, splashing in the waves in her pink bikini, so carefree, and let out a sigh. Would she ever get to see things like that again? Would she, Kelsey, and Aiden, ever be a family again?

Right now, it felt like a faraway, impossible dream.

She closed the door, kicked off her shoes, and walked across the cold, threadbare carpeting, unbuttoning her jeans. She slipped out of them, then took off her bra under her t-shirt. She'd sleep in that shirt, since she only had one more clean shirt in her bag. She'd have to figure out a way to do laundry soon, and not in the sink.

Truthfully, she was too tired and sad to bother.

Throwing her hair into a messy bun, she pulled back the comforter and sat in the bed, turning on the television to keep her company. Some awful reality television show was playing, where people were arguing. She turned to the news, then to a cartoon. It was the only thing that didn't depress her further.

You know, Mia, what the only way to get out a funk is, don't you? DO SOMETHING.

She sighed. Then she grabbed her phone and plugged it in. She found the hotel's Wi-Fi password and connected to the internet, then started her research.

First, she looked for any breaking news about the murders. There was nothing more than the article she'd seen in the newspaper. Nothing about a possible murder-suicide. Maybe the police were still making the case for that one.

Then, she Googled the victims, Kiki Redbone and Jason Delaney-Sawyer. That brought about a flurry of results. Kiki had won a Democracy in America essay contest as a freshman, had been promoted to captain of the varsity cheer squad for her senior year at Oak Cliff, and participated in track, running a mile in under seven minutes. Jason was also a runner, and had gone to Houston last year and come in third in the State Science Fair. It was just like Tori and River had said—these kids were squeaky clean, All-American.

Then how had they ended up dead?

There must've been something else to it. Mia snuggled deeper under the covers and scrolled through more. This time, she entered in Tori Schloss and River Alvarez. She got more high school accomplishments, National Honor Society memberships, yearbook editor appointments, lead in the school play, awards of all kinds.

Nothing of interest.

But then she looked up Bronson Shu. That came up with something interesting.

A previous arrest, right when he turned eighteen. For assault. Shu's mugshot was frightening, cold. Mia clicked on the article, but it was caught behind a firewall, so she couldn't read the rest of it.

Assault. So that meant he had a violent streak . . . which could mean that he was worth looking into some more.

She wasn't too sure his alibi was rock-solid. Had he somehow falsified the logbook at the gym, gotten the owners there to lie on his behalf?

But then whose footprints were those, leading away from the crime scene? She wasn't absolutely sure, but they didn't look like Shu's.

She groaned. If only she could look into what the police had. Cell phone records. The murder weapon. Something. She felt like she was working with a puzzle that was missing a bunch of pieces. Not only that, she was so exhausted, she could barely see straight.

Yawning, she set her phone on the night table, turned off the light, and in yet another new and uncomfortable bed, tried to find a good night's sleep.

*

Mia was in a park with her family on a beautiful summer's day, lying on a soft blanket in the electric-green grass, the fragrance of flowers and fresh air strong in her nostrils. Insects buzzed in her ears. The sky was bright blue, the sun was strong and high overhead, and the birds were singing happily nearby. There was a warm, relaxing feeling of peace inside her, one that told her all would be okay.

"Mommy," Kelsey said, snuggling next to her. "There's an ice cream truck. Can I have a strawberry shortcake pop?"

She smiled without opening her eyes. She didn't want this perfect moment to get away. "You just had lunch. Maybe later."

Her daughter huffed. "But mom. I'm hungry *now*. And he's leaving."

Mia was about to say, *Oh, well, all right then.* Aiden must've known, because he chuckled and shifted beside her, then pulled away.

"That's okay, string bean. I'll get you one." She could hear him fishing in his pockets for change. "Come on."

She heard the sound of their feet, swishing through the grass, away from her, and sucked in a breath of warm summer air. She was so drowsy and content, she felt like she could sleep there, forever, happily.

But then she saw the darkness behind her eyelids. A cold breeze swept through, plucking up goose bumps on her arms. She cracked an eye and saw dark storm clouds, rolling in. Above her, lightning flashed.

In a blink, she sat up, looking for her family. She saw Kelsey and her husband, standing by the ice cream cart, only a few yards away. Aiden was frozen, facing the ice cream man, his back to her. As the first raindrops began to fall, Kelsey looked back at her, suddenly frightened. "Mommy?" she said, her voice trembling.

Above, thunder boomed, making everything shake.

When Mia took a step in her daughter's direction, the space between them started to stretch and distort like a funhouse mirror. She took another, then another, but the more steps she took, the more it seemed to stretch, until Kelsey was just a spot in the distance.

Kelsey began to scream. "Mommy!"

"I'm coming," Mia shouted, hysterical, taking giant leaps in effort to get to her. Not that it did any good. Now, Kelsey was standing on a curb.

The boom of thunder changed to a different sound. The blaring of a horn, and suddenly something—many somethings—rushed between her and her daughter.

Cars.

She was standing in the median of a massive, California-sized, multi-lane freeway. Around her, cars barreled by at breakneck speed, some flashing their lights, some laying on their horns. Rain was falling harder now, blurring everything. Cars whizzed by, mere inches from her.

"Kelsey!" she screamed, but her voice seemed to die inside her. Across the highway, she could no longer see her daughter.

But she could hear her. She was crying, every sob twisting Mia's heart tighter. "Mommy!" Kelsey screamed again, and this time, Mia saw her. She looked so fragile, so alone, standing there on the edge of the curb.

"Don't move, I'm coming for you," she shouted, watching the cars rush by, looking for an opening. Impossible. There was no opening. She'd never make it. She was stuck.

“Mommy, I can’t,” Kelsey sobbed, watching the traffic, too. “I need you.”

Mia saw the change in her expression. She knew exactly what was in her daughter’s eyes. Determination. She was going to make a run for it.

“Kelsey, no!” she screamed in desperation, as her daughter took the first step into the roadway . . .

Mia sat straight up in bed, her heart pounding, sheets damp with her sweat. She looked around, taking in the cheesy seventies furnishings of the old hotel room she’d checked into last night, and heaved a sigh of relief.

Just a dream. And yet, it made her shudder. What kind of life was her nine-year-old daughter living, now, without a mother? She knew Aiden was doing his best, and her parents were probably pitching in where they good, but that couldn’t compensate for a mom. If she’d been in prison, at least, she could visit Kelsey, have phone calls with her. But being on the run? She hadn’t spoken to Kelsey in months. And she couldn’t have any contact with her, either. It was too dangerous.

Her heart ached at the thought of doing irreparable damage to her daughter. She heard the same bullshit time and time again. *Kids are resilient. They’ll be fine.* But there was only so much a kid could take. And Kelsey had been through the ringer.

She fell back to her pillow and stared at the ceiling in the darkness. How much more could Kelsey withstand? How much more could she withstand? What if she never got her life back? A timebomb was ticking, and she had no idea when it would go off.

She tried to fall back to sleep, but with those thoughts cycling through her mind, it wasn’t possible. She hated inaction. She needed to do something. But what? She’d been beating her head against a wall for so long, never finding the way in.

She rolled over in bed and looked at the clock. Four in the morning. Sighing, she got out of bed to take a shower, hoping that it would bring her clarity. A way out. Something that could help her to get home.

CHAPTER ELEVEN

The Canton Gas 'n' Go Travel Mall was a stop on the highway, directly across from the Horizon Motel where Mia had stayed. She'd been so tired the night before that she hadn't really noticed it, despite its huge size and the crowds of truckers using it as a resting spot for the night. When she stepped outside, looking for a fast-food place to grab a bite to eat, the restaurant's sign caught her eye. *Tired of Fast Food? Try some of Momma's Flapjacks. Made with Love.*

She almost laughed. Tired of fast food? They had no idea. Her stomach was forever rebelling, these days, because of the dozens of meals she'd gotten from the drive-thru.

Even if it probably wasn't true, the advertisement won her over. She walked across to the Travel Mall and went inside.

Mia had expected a greasy spoon diner, just like the many she'd been in before, but she was wrong. The small restaurant looked like an old grandmother's formal dining room, only slightly larger, with several mismatched tables all over. There was a big brick fireplace on one side, pink wallpaper, and Texas décor—steer horns, Texas flags, rusting farm implements—over all the walls. A waitress in a pink apron smiled at her. "Hey y'all. I'm Momma. Table for one?"

Mia smiled back. "That's right."

"Well, you come right on over here, Honey. We've got a place for you."

She brought her to a darling table in the corner, next to front windows with lace, ruffled curtains. "Thanks," Mia said as she took the menu. "I really would like some of your flapjacks."

"Coming right up! And some extra strong coffee? Maybe some bacon?" The woman said sweetly in a deep drawl.

"Sounds good."

Momma walked off, leaving her to look around the place. Though many trucks had been parked outside, the place was empty, except for a trio of truckers, eating their breakfasts and talking loudly. Mia's stomach grumbled at the sight of the food; she hadn't realized how hungry she was.

Two of the men were facing toward her, talking so much that the speed they were shoveling pancakes into their mouths was quite impressive. They were wearing dirty jeans, and one had full sleeves of tattoos on his scrawny biceps. His black hair was so greasy that it seemed to drip out from underneath his trucker's cap. His laugh was almost comical. "Haw, haw, haw," he ground out. "I ain't been home in thirty-six weeks . . . and counting."

"That's too bad," the other man, said, wiping syrup from his long, frizzy brown beard. He was so plump that his belly barely fit under the table, and his cheeks so round that his eyes looked perpetually closed.

"Nah, it ain't. Don't want to go back to the old lady's nagging. She nags me even when I ain't there." He laughed some more.

The other man, the one facing away from them, grunted. "I hear you on that one. I once took a trip up to New York just to get away from mine. Ain't no one who likes driving a truck into New York City. But I done it, more than enough times, to get away from her."

"That's right." The tattooed man pounded the newspaper. "That's why I think this story's a load of bull. Ain't no one killing their girl and turning the gun on themselves, unless they're married. This guy was free and clear. Most men in that state would be out celebrating."

Mia leaned forward, trying to see the newspaper article. Were they talking about the Jacob Delaney-Sawyer case? Had the police finally announced that Jacob was a suspect? She couldn't see, so she grabbed her phone and looked it up.

Sure enough, the first article she saw said: *POLICE EYEING MURDER-SUICIDE IN DEATH OF LOOKOUT POINT COUPLE.*

She bit her lip. Poor Linda. This would gut her. And it was wrong. Mia wondered if she should have warned her this might happen.

"Police are dumb as a box of rocks if that's what they think," the bearded man said. "You'd think some of them would look into ties to that case out of Canton."

Canton. That town was about twenty miles south, about an hour east of Dallas. It was known as the town with the biggest flea market in the country. She'd been there, once, before Kelsey was born, to buy baby furniture for her nursery. It seemed like ages ago that she was walking up and down the aisles of that massive flea market, looking for a diamond in the rough she could transform into a changing table for Kelsey's bedroom. Aiden had been so worried that she might give birth in the middle of it all, since she was about eight-months pregnant. She'd constantly nudged him off, saying she was fine, in that "nesting" period where she had a burst of energy and wanted to fix up the house for their new bundle of joy.

She swallowed back the bittersweet memory, blinking back tears that threatened to come into her eyes. Canton was a nice town. What had happened there?

She plugged it in, but nothing came up.

"You okay, Honey?" a voice said. It was Momma, stopping at her table to fill a mug of coffee for her.

"Yep, great," she said, managing a smile as she looked up from her phone, still trying to think of good keywords to use.

"Cream? Sugar?"

"Just black, thanks," she said, typing in *Murder suicide Canton.*

Still nothing.

"Your breakfast will be right out," she said, as the men at the table next to her broke out in laughter.

"Thanks," she said absently, trying to eavesdrop again to get more information.

"But I'm a lot fatter than that!" the chubby one said, patting his belly.

Great. They've moved on, she thought, wondering if she'd missed anything. If she was going to find out more about the Canton case, she'd have to take matters into her own hands.

She stood up and stepped towards their table, standing between them. "Excuse me," she said kindly. "I just happened to overhear you mention something about a murder . . ."

They stopped laughing and looked at her. There was silence until the tattooed man dropped his fork on his plate and raised both hands in surrender. "It wasn't me! I swear!"

More laughter. The fat man pounded the table with a fist, his face turning red. She waited for them to calm down and said, "Oh, I know. But it did interest me. I heard about the murder of those kids in the area of Lookout Point, from the paper. You said there's another case that's similar?"

The tattooed man wiped his mouth with a napkin. "That's right. Over in Canton. Couple of teens wound up dead. Both shot in the head. They said it was some kind of suicide pact on that one, too." He shook his head. "Now I know teens are all sorts of crazy in the head these days, but to me, it sounds a little fishy. If I were the police, I'd be looking into it."

"Funny, I never saw any mention of it online," she said, typing in *Suicide Pact – Canton.*

Sure enough, an article appeared. *Two Canton Teens Dead in Suspected Suicide Pact.*

There it was.

Two teens found dead in a suspected suicide pact at a nature reserve have been identified.

The bodies of Tobias Williams, 18, and Mariana Powell, 17, were discovered at Two Acre Lake Nature Reserve, near Canton, by a dog walker last week.

Information released by the Canton coroner's office said Mr. Williams and Miss Powell were both from the area and attended Canton High School together.

Canton Police said the deaths are not being treated as suspicious but investigators are trying to establish the circumstances on behalf of the coroner. "We are currently assessing the available information to determine what further action may be required from us."

In an appeal for information last week, police described Tobias as white, around 5ft 7in, of slim build and with short, dark hair, a short beard and brown eyes. He was wearing brown lace-up boots, light gray sweatpants, a dark t-shirt and a navy hoodie.

Mariana was also white, around 5ft 5in, of slim build with dark brown, shoulder-length hair and brown eyes. She was wearing black and white running shoes, light gray sweatpants, a navy t-shirt.

Police Detective Simon Charles, of the Canton Police, said: "Our thoughts are with the families and friends of the two young people who tragically died."

As Mia read the whole article, everything around her fell away, until one of the men at the table cleared his throat. She realized they were all staring at her. She pointed to it. "Found the article. But it doesn't say . . .you don't think it's a suicide?"

The tattooed guy shrugged. "Maybe. Maybe not. I'll tell you, I think it's a little odd that these two couples died a week apart. Don't you?"

She shrugged. "Doesn't say how they died . . .?"

"They were shot," the man with the beard said.

That piqued Mia's interest. "Really? How do you know?"

"Because I read it in an article somewhere. The gun was left at the scene."

That was interesting. She was pretty sure she'd heard the same about the case in Dallas. The gun was left there, which was why it had looked like a murder-suicide. She looked over at the other man, who nodded. "I read the same. Damn shame, happening to those kids, in the prime of their lives. They hardly got to living yet."

Mia nodded thoughtfully. "So if you don't think it's murder-suicide, what do you think could've happened to them?"

Bearded man took a gulp of his coffee and raised a finger. "What I think is that there's some yahoo running around who doesn't like these kids. Maybe he envies their youth or something like that. Whatever it is, he's just sick enough that he don't want 'em living no more. So he kills 'em."

"Honey?"

Mia turned to find Momma standing behind her, face white as a sheet. She had a curious look on her face. "I don't know if I want to know what y'all are discussing. Doesn't sound very pleasant to me."

"Oh, we were just—"

"Your breakfast is ready," Momma said, moving aside to reveal the largest plate of pancakes Mia had ever seen, still steaming, a square of butter melting into the top. It was sitting at her place setting, next to an assortment of syrups.

"Wow, that's big," she said, sitting down in her seat. "You're going to need a truck to move me after this, but it looks really gr—"

"You were talking about the Canton kids who died, right?" Momma said, leaning in, her brow creased with worry.

"Yes . . . they were saying they don't think they are suicides. That they might be related to the deaths that happened at Lookout Point, after that carnival?"

Momma shrugged. "Well, I don't know about that. But I do agree about them not being suicides. I know Mari's mom, Katty Powell. She was beside herself when her daughter died. She was going places, that girl, Mari. She was accepted to college. Tulane. And she was excited about it. She never gave them any hint of a thought that she was depressed. And that boy? She'd only been dating him a couple weeks! Suicide pact? Her momma didn't think so at all." She shook her head.

"Did Katty Powell tell the police that?"

She nodded. "Oh, she tried. Didn't do much good. They wanted to wrap it up with a little bow, put it on the shelf, so they did."

"And this boy, Tobias Williams? You don't think that maybe she didn't know him well, and he murdered her, then turned the gun on himself?"

"Nope," Momma said. "Katty didn't think so. He was going places, too. He was in his first year at college, and a real nice kid. It was only their second date, of course, but Katty's a pretty strict lady. If she had any reason to believe he wasn't going to take care of her girl Mari, she'd have kicked him out on his ear. She was always very careful about who she let Mari see. And this boy passed with flying colors."

Mia opened her phone and wrote down *Katty Powell, Mariana Powell, Tobias Williams, Two Acre Lake Nature Preserve,* for future reference.

"Well," Momma said, tapping the table with a sharp, pink-painted fingernail. "I'll let you get to eatin' before it gets cold. You let me know if you need somethin', all right, Honey?"

Mia nodded, placed a napkin on her lap, and set into eating the giant stack of pancakes. As she did, she stared at the names of the teen victims. Was it possible that the murder of Jacob and Kiki was part of a serial killing?

She didn't know, but now she had a lead. Two Acre Lake Nature Preserve, the scene of the first murders. She'd have to check it out.

CHAPTER TWELVE

Two Acre Lake wasn't really a Nature Preserve, with miles upon miles of rolling lands to get lost in. "Nature Preserve" was far too lofty a name for it. It was a park with a small lake, right off the main road, with lots of reeds and a small dock, stretching into the middle of the calm, dark waters. There were a couple of kids playing in the water, and a few kayakers in the middle of the calm lake, as well as a fisherman or two casting lines. But other than that, the place wasn't exactly a hotspot. Mia easily found a parking spot in the gravel lot off the road, and stepped out of the car, trying to determine exactly where the bodies had been found.

Mia walked around a dirt trail until she came to the telltale police tape, by the Mill Creek Reservoir. The tape hadn't been well maintained, because there were just a few wisps of it, caught among the reeds and blowing in the wind.

As Mia was staring at it, trying to determine just where the two young people had met their ends, a high voice said, "Are you another YouTuber?"

She looked around and saw a little kid, maybe twelve or so, with a shaggy bowl-shaped haircut, falling in his eyes so that he had to tilt his head back to see her. He was as skinny as a reed and holding a fishing rod, his jeans rolled up to his knees, feet stuck in the edge of the water.

Surprised, she took a step back, then relaxed when she realized he didn't pose much of a threat. "No, I'm—"

"You're looking into those people who got killed here," he said with a grin. "I can always tell. Because you don't look like you're here to fish or swim. And that's all anyone ever came here for, before. So are you taking video?"

She shook her head. "I'm—"

"If you are, can I be in it? Maybe I can be famous. You can interview me."

She smiled. "Sorry. No. I'm not taking video."

"Oh. Darn." He snapped his fingers. "I like them videos. You know, like the ones that say, 'Places where people were last seen alive.'

Or 'Haunted locations.' So wait. Are you like, police or something like that?"

"Yeah. Something like that." She sat on a rock behind him and watched him cast his line into the water. "You're fishing, hmm?"

"Brilliant observation," he said with a laugh. "Yeah, I fish here every chance I get. Which isn't really that often. I'm in the seventh grade. I got homework up the butt. But every afternoon, when I'm done, I'm here."

"You fish here that often?" This was good. The kid was bright and observant. Maybe he knew something about the deaths of those two people. "Catch anything?"

"A cold, maybe." He laughed, "Yeah, sometimes I catch a fish or two. I love doing it. Been doing it since I was a baby."

She motioned to the tape. "Do a lot of people come out here, looking for the place where those people died?"

He nodded and cast his line again. "Yep. All the time. Mostly people younger than you, though. They take video for their channels, thinking they're going to be famous one day, or whatever. But they might as well just lie and show off a pile of dirt, not like anyone else would know the difference. There's nothing there, nothing like a bloody spot or brains smeared all over the ground. Just a bunch of reeds."

She tilted her head and peered through the thick reeds, which were almost as tall as she was. "In there, right?" she pointed, and he nodded. "You looked?"

"Of course. I didn't find the bodies or else I would've pooped myself, probably. Lady walking her dog did that, because they were in the reeds right by the reservoir and he must've sniffed them out. But I showed up right when the police came. They wouldn't let me get to my spot, but I saw them fishing the bodies out of the reeds. It was pretty dope."

"Dope?" She raised an eyebrow.

He shrugged. "Okay, it was pretty gruesome and gave me nightmares for a week. They put sheets over the bodies when they pulled them out but the one fell off as they were moving the girl. They'd been in the water for a while so she was all white and bloated. She looked like, uh, you know, one of those manatees, or a whale. You know? Her skin looked like paste." He made a face.

Mia smiled. It was the same face Kelsey used to make whenever she got grossed out. "Really, so it happened a while ago, then . . ."

"It's probably been a week and a half since they were killed. A few days since they were pulled out of there, at least. I don't know. I just hear people talking. They come here with their phone cameras and say, 'This is it. This is where the suicide pact was carried out.'" He shook his head. "Not that I believe any of that horsecocky."

"You don't?"

"Nope. I knew the boy, Tobias. Not well, but we passed the time of day. He went to school with my older brother. He wasn't the type." He tilted his head. "I guess people always say that. *I never thought he had it in him.* But really, with Tobias? It's the God's-honest truth. Never been a better kid than him. Thought he was going to go off, and one day we'd learn he cured cancer. He was the brightest. Going places. If he was depressed or under stress, you'd never know it. Not him."

She nodded and looked around. The area was isolated, and far away from the main road. If the bodies had been found in the reeds, she had to admit, that was a strange place to carry out a suicide pact. It made more sense that someone would've followed them there, killed them, then dragged them into the lake.

Or maybe not.

Jacob and Kiki's bodies had been found in a clearing, outside of the woods, which was a place that wasn't heavily traveled. Had they been dragged out there, too? Mia hadn't seen any signs of dragging, but she'd been so busy looking at footprints. And by the time she'd gotten there, there'd been plenty of those, mostly from police officers. Maybe the bodies had been dragged there in effort to hide them. If that was the case, how could the police think it was anything other than a murder?

Whoever had done this had been careful not to leave any tracks. Then what about those tracks she'd seen, leading away from the other crime scene?

Maybe they meant nothing.

Meaning she was back to square one.

But this little boy . . . something told Mia he was a wealth of information. "Hey. What's your name?"

The kid squinted. "Well, I'm not supposed to talk to strangers, but you look pretty normal. I'm Danny."

She reached over and shook his hand. "I'm Mi—" She stopped. She'd been so comfortable talking to the little boy that she'd forgotten her troubles. "Mimi."

"Mimi?" He laughed. "Cool name."

"Yeah. So, Danny," she started, not really sure where she was headed with the line of questioning. "You must hear the talk, if you knew Tobias. People are talking about it, right? What does everyone think? Not suicide?"

He nodded. "Yep. When the police came to that conclusion we all thought it was crazy."

"All right. Then what do they think happened?"

"They have their weird theories. Some people thought it was road rage. He accidentally pissed off the wrong guy, who followed him here. We got a lot of road ragers around here."

"Is that what you think?"

He shook his head. "No. I think it was the Cackling Man."

"The Cackling Man?"

He nodded. "Guy's always showing up around here. I think he's homeless. And you know when he's coming because he's laughing. But not in a nice way. It sounds like a cackle. He wears a coat, even in the summer, and usually he has the collar up real high so you can't see his face. He's always around, just watching."

"Really?" She looked around. "Where is he now?"

"He usually hides out under the bridge on the other side of the lake. I think that's where he sleeps. But sometimes he walks around, and I see him, laughing and muttering to himself." The little boy shuddered.

"Has he ever threatened you?"

Danny nodded. "He told me if he saw me around here again, he'd kill me."

"And that didn't frighten you?"

He shrugged. "He's told me that about twenty times. But he never does anything. Sometimes he throws rocks at me, but other than that, he keeps his distance."

"But aren't you worried, now that those bodies were found?"

"Not really."

"Why not?"

"Because they pulled the gun out of the reeds with the bodies. And The Cackling Man doesn't strike me as someone who carries a bunch of weapons on him. He probably found the gun somewhere, used it, and dumped it. So I think he's still harmless." He shrugged. "Plus, even with all his yelling and screaming, I think he kind of likes me. But he doesn't like people like *them*."

"Like the couple who died?"

“Right. He chased a few couples away, more than once. It’s pretty funny to watch,” he laughed.

“Is it?”

“Yeah. They’re being gross, all kissy and lovey-dovey, and the next thing you know, they’re running for their lives!” He laughed more, so hard he had to hold his belly. “Classic.”

“Have you ever seen him go after anyone else?”

Danny squinted, looking up at the sky, thinking. “Don’t know. Hmm, I’m trying to remember.” He stepped out of the water and reached into a bucket, pulling out a couple more worms, which he attached to the hook. “Yeah. There’s been a few people who said he might have picked their pockets and stuff while they’re not looking. But he looks kind of scary so most people usually steer clear of him when they see him coming.”

She pulled her legs up under her and stood up on the rock. Shielding her eyes from the sun with her hand, she gazed over the smooth surface of the lake. There were a few kayakers in the distance, and some low-hanging trees obscuring the view. “Where’s this bridge you were talking about?”

“On the other side of the lake.”

She glanced down at him. “You think he’s there now?”

The kid’s jaw dropped. “What . . . are you gonna go talk to him?”

She nodded.

“Wow, lady, you’re brave,” he said, digging his pole into the ground and skipping down the path a little ways. “Yeah, he’s probably there right now. He stays under the bridge when it’s really hot, like some kind of troll. I think if you go this way, it’s faster.”

“Great, thanks,” she said, sliding off the rock and heading up the bank, toward the path. “I appreciate your help, Danny.”

“Wait!” he called after her, rushing to grab his pole and bucket. “Can I come with you? I don’t want to miss this!”

She held up a hand. “No, it could be trouble. I think you should stay here and keep fishing. Looks like you might have a bite.”

He looked down at his pole. Sure enough, the line was taut, and bobbing a little bit. “Whoo hoo!” he shouted, running toward it, shoving his hair out of his eyes. He grabbed the pole with both hands and started to reel it in. “Feels like a big one! I bet it’s a shark!”

“Good luck,” she said, heading toward the bridge, trying not to think too much about the one time she, Aiden, and Kelsey went fishing at a pond near her house. Aiden had bought hundreds of dollars’ worth of fishing equipment, and they'd wound up sunburned and without a single bite, because Kelsey had cried the entire time.

The bridge was quite the hike, around the far side of the lake. It crossed over a shallow place, separating the lake from a smaller pool. As she neared it, she saw a pair of old shoes and a ratty blanket, laid out near one side of the bridge. She climbed down the bank and peered underneath, into the darkness. There was no one there.

She sighed and was about to turn back when a voice said, "What the hell are you doing, snooping around my home? I'll slit your throat if you try to steal from me!"

And then came an awful cackle, so loud that it scraped against her eardrums and made every hair on the back of her neck stand at attention.

CHAPTER THIRTEEN

Mia held up both her hands to show she was unarmed, and slowly turned around. "Hello," she said pleasantly, "Mr . . ."

Mr Cackling Man was all that came to mind as she looked into the eyes of the man. He wasn't nearly as frightening as she'd expected. Based on Danny's description, she'd been expecting a male version of the Wicked Witch of the West, complete with green skin, hooked, wart-covered nose and pointed hat. But the Cackling Man was a skinny, old man with a grizzled face, covered in whiskers and deep wrinkles. His gray hair was long and curled around his ears, and from the way his lips stretched, she could tell he was missing teeth. His eyes were wild, sprinting all over the place, and he smelled like the inside of a wine cask. He was drunk.

"I wasn't going to take your things . . . I'm sorry. What's your name?" she said, trying to be amicable.

"Smitty," he said, pushing past her and heading for his place. As he moved, he breathed on her, and the odor nearly knocked her over. "Sure you weren't. You expect me to believe that? Everyone around here's after something from me. This is my home, and they keep coming to it."

"It's a public park," she pointed out.

"And I been coming here longer than anyone. It's mine," he snapped, and as he did, she realized he had few teeth left. The one he had on top was nearly black. "And you're trespassing."

"I just came to talk to you."

He climbed under the bridge, and for a moment, disappeared in the shadows. Then he poked his head out, focusing one eye on her. "About what?"

From the surprise on his face, she got the feeling that no one ever talked to him. Danny had said he scared people away, which made her a little sad. "Oh, I figured you probably know a lot about the goings on in this park, since it's yours and all. Am I right?"

He nodded. "Yeah. I know everything about this place."

"You know Danny, then, do you? The little boy?"

He nodded. "That little whippersnapper? Oh, yeah, he's trouble, that one. I gotta keep my eye on him. He makes it look like he's fishing, but he's always looking around, waiting for me to put my guard down so he can come and steal my stuff."

"Your stuff?"

His eyes narrowed. "I'm not showing you, neither. You'd want to steal it, too."

She held out both hands. "Oh, no. I promise I wouldn't. I'm just interested in the goings on around this park. I guess you noticed the excitement here, a couple weeks ago?"

He frowned and seemed to shrink away, back under the bridge. "Nope. I didn't notice anything."

He's lying. "Really?"

"Yeah. Who's asking?" He studied her closely, suspicious.

She needed to find another tack. "Like I said, I just wanted to talk. I'm actually a journalist. I'm doing a piece on this park, and I thought there was no one better to get the inside scoop on it than from you, since you know it so well."

His eyes went wide. "A piece? Like an article?"

She nodded.

"You mean, like for a magazine or something?"

"Sure," she lied.

"Well, why didn't you say so?" he said, his demeanor changing in an instant. "Come in, come in. Sit down."

She wasn't sure she wanted to, considering it didn't look very clean under that bridge, and it probably wasn't safe to be in the darkness with a possible killer. But this man clearly had a couple of screws loose, and right now, he was her best suspect. Her only suspect. "All right," she said, ducking her head and climbing under the bridge.

"Take this," he said, handing her a dusty round chair cushion. "Sit anywhere. Anywhere you like."

She took it, allowing her eyes to adjust to the darkness, and found a place, far enough away from him that if he made any sudden movements, she'd be prepared. She placed the cushion on the stony terrain, and as she sat down, she noticed some of his things he was so intent on her not taking—he had a small camping burner, a worn bedroll, and a canvas bag, stuffed full—of what, she couldn't tell.

"Thanks," she said.

"You going to take my picture?" he said, fluffing the greasy hair around his ears like a debutante.

“Sure.” She took out her phone and snapped a few photos as he turned and preened, smiling that near-toothless smile. She checked the photos. *Well, if I die, and anyone finds my phone, they’ll know who killed me.* “These are great.”

Pocketing her phone, she pulled her knees up, crisscross-applesauce.

“So, you know everything about this place. And you don’t know about the incident that happened a couple weeks ago. I find that hard to believe.”

His face fell. “I already told you.”

“Are you sure? There must’ve been a lot of police cars here. Those two bodies they found? You didn’t see them? And the gunshots that went off must’ve echoed all through here. You didn’t hear them?”

He shook his head wildly. “Nope, nope, nope. I didn’t hear or see any of that. I must’ve been asleep. I don’t know nothing about any of that.”

“Oh. And you don’t know of any reports of people having their pockets picked while they’re at the park, enjoying it?”

More head-shaking. “No. Not at all. Unless you count all the people that have been trying to steal from *me*.” He looked back at his little trove of junk. “What are you, girl? Are you some kind of private detective or something? Why you come asking me all these questions? You’re not welcome in my place.”

Once again, she held up her hands to appease him. “No, like I said, I’m a journalist, working on—"

“Get out.”

“Smitty,” she began. “I just want to—”

Her breath caught in her throat as he reached into his bag and pulled out a long, rusty butcher’s knife. “Get. Out,” he snarled, pointing it at her.

“You don’t need that,” she said, trying to get to her feet, her intuition buzzing inside her, telling her she couldn’t just leave. If this man was pulling a knife on her, there was something he didn’t want her finding out. Maybe he had killed those people.

One thing was sure. She wasn’t going to leave until she made absolutely sure.

He jabbed the knife toward her. “All right, all right, I’m going,” she said, moving toward the underside of the bridge. She stooped like she was about to go out, but then, brought her arm back, catching Smitty unaware. She grabbed the wrist of the hand wielding the weapon and twisted it hard, so hard that he dropped the knife.

He grunted as she wrenched his arm around, pulling it behind his back, and shoving him face-forward to the ground. Pulling his arm back hard, she leaned over and whispered, “I don’t want any of your junk. I just want answers.”

Smitty wailed. “I don’t got none! I don’t know nothing about crimes happening here!”

“Bullshit. You’re here all the time. You must’ve seen something.”

He sniffled. She couldn’t see his face, buried in the dirt, but it sounded like he was crying. “Okay, maybe I saw something! Maybe I took a few wallets and things from people. But that was when I thought they just left it here, I thought they didn’t want it. If you let me go, I’ll give it all back. I promise.”

That explained why he was so wary of her. But was there more? She didn’t loosen her grip. “The murders, Smitty. What about them? Did you see the couple who got murdered across the pond?”

He shook his head. “No. No, I didn’t do that. I don’t know who did!”

“Did you see them?”

He swallowed, and nodded slightly. ”Yeah. I guess I did. I saw them heading from the lot to the path. I thought it was weird because they never came back. Their car was there overnight. When I went looking for them later, they were gone. I didn’t hear no gunshots.”

“Did you see anyone else around there? Anyone else who might’ve looked out of place? Who you’d never seen before?”

“There were a lot of people who I’d never seen before, back then. It always gets that way during the carnival.”

She blinked and loosened her hold on him. “Carnival? What carnival?”

“It was the weekend of the Canton annual carnival. It’s held on the grounds next door. So a lot of people come by here to walk around the park. I don’t keep track of all of ‘em.”

She let go of him. He scrambled up and grabbed his bag, thrusting it over to her.

“Here. Take it. I don’t want it. You can have it all.”

She opened the drawstring and looked inside. She found a few trinkets, jewelry, a couple of leather billfolds. She opened them and found the IDs. They belonged to other people. As an officer of the law, she’d have tried to get them back to who they belonged to. Now, she couldn't do anything with them. She tossed it over to him. "Do you remember anything else about that couple?"

He started to shake his head, but then his eyes lit up. "I remember. They were arguing."

"About what?"

He shrugged. "I don't know. She said something about how she didn't care about it, and then she ran off, and he followed behind her."

Mia frowned. "That's it?"

He nodded. "I promise. I don't know nothing else."

"I hope you'll stay here, in case I have any other questions," she said, turning to leave. "And don't go stealing from other people again."

As she ducked her head out from under the bridge and blinked in the bright sunlight, a voice said, "Wow, that was super cool! The way you knocked his block off? I never saw anyone do that!"

She climbed the bank to where Danny was standing. "Didn't I tell you to stay put?"

"Sorry. I lost the fish," he said with a shrug. "Are you a ninja? How did you level him like that? That was some crazy Kung Fu stuff!"

He started to act it out, adding a kick and a "Hi-Ya!" for effect.

She shook her head and walked past him. "Let's just keep this between you and me right now, okay?"

He nodded. "Sure thing. I wouldn't want to be on your bad side, Mimi."

She walked back to the parking lot and slid into the front seat of her car, her mind playing over one thing Smitty had said. *It was the weekend of the Canton annual carnival. It's held on the grounds next door.*

Kiki had also mentioned a carnival, being held by the grounds next to Lookout Point.

It might have just been a coincidence, but it was something. And as she put her car into reverse, she decided to look into it.

CHAPTER FOURTEEN

The sound of the calliope on the merry-go-round lilted in the breezeless, hot air, buffeted now and again by cries of glee. Everywhere, balloons floated, the sweet scent of funnel cake lofted, and children ran around with their cotton candy and ice cream treats, excitedly pointing out which rides they wanted to try, as their parents tried to keep up.

The man stood in the grass by the entrance to the Zipper. He liked filling in here. It wasn't ever busy. A couple of kids with bright-green wristbands looked up at it, eyes wide in amazement.

"You coming on?" he asked, holding open the gate for them.

The bravest of the two took a step forward, until a polo-wearing father reached out and clamped a hand over his shoulder. "I don't think so, Sport," the father said. "That one's a little too rough for you."

"Aw, Dad! I'm brave!" the boy said, licking his lips.

"Ah, it's not so bad," the man said, reaching for the yardstick to check the boy's height. "If you reach this point, you can ride."

The man held it up to the tallest of the boys. He straightened his spine as high as he could, but it wasn't enough. The man snapped his fingers. "Too bad, kid. You're about an inch too short."

The father shrugged and led the kids away, toward the Cyclone.

It was the early-bird special. Parents were treating their little kids, just off from school, to an afternoon of fun. Pay one price for a wristband, and it was all-you-could-ride until seven p.m. Or, as the carnies called it, afternoon break, at least for the Zipper operator. Young kids usually stayed away from the Zipper. It was serious business, as the riders sat in a cage that spun upside down and around, while the entire ride spun in another direction. Even most adults couldn't stomach it and stayed away.

So he had the afternoon to watch, and wait. And observe.

As he sat back on the metal stool buried in the thick grass, behind the control panel, he watched a girl and her boyfriend. Teens. They were sitting together on stools at the Blow Up, the race where you had to shoot a gun to blow up a balloon, and the first person who popped the balloon won a prize. She was wearing a tight tank top and short shorts, exposing her tanned limbs and belly, her blonde hair piled on her head in a messy loop. He was wearing baggy jeans, a tight t-shirt, and a backwards baseball cap. They'd been here for a while, had likely cut school to come. So intent were they on winning that they didn't notice him watching them.

"I'm going to get you, Marcus!" she screamed.

"Uh-uh, I got this. You're toast, G."

It brought him back to his own youth, a decade ago. When he was so young and foolish and wanted nothing more than a beautiful girl to marry, to grow old with. It was his big romantic fantasy, stealing kisses with the love of his life at the very top of the Ferris wheel, while the whole world lay at their feet, unaware of what they were up to. All those years of grabbing a cotton candy and taking the ride to the top of the wheel himself, he'd waited for that moment. He could think of nothing he'd rather do than adore and take care of his woman, for the rest of his life, starting with that one, precious moment.

How many girls from high school had he invited to accompany him? Twelve? Twenty? They all seemed to meld together, into one. Because they'd all turned him down.

So he'd continued to take that ride, up to the top of the wheel, again and again, growing more and more bitter, every time.

Until he broke.

Suddenly, the balloon popped, and a bell went off. "And we have a winner!" the barker announced, as Marcus raised his arms in a victory V. "Anything from the third shelf."

He tapped his chin, thinking, and G gave him a look. "The pink flamingo! The flamingo," she begged. "You know that's my favorite animal, Marcus, dummy!"

He nodded and motioned to it, and the barker brought it down and handed it to her. She cradled it in her arms like a child and gave it a kiss on the beak. "You owe me, big-time, Gianna," the kid said as he put an arm around her and dragged her to the next display.

Oh, now, they would be perfect. Marcus and Gianna. Together, forever.

He swallowed. No. He had to wait. He'd killed too quickly, the last time. First Canton. Then Lookout Point. He'd meant to wait a month, but he just couldn't resist. Those two geeky kids were so in love, so full of themselves that they noticed nothing else but themselves. It made it easy. Sometimes, the opportunity was too perfect.

Like these kids.

They caught sight of his ride at the same time, and Gianna tugged on Marcus's arm. "Oh, the Zipper! I love that one."

He shook his head. "Nah—"

"What are you, scared?" She grabbed his hand and pulled him toward the gate, where the man sat. She ran through the gate, barely noticing him, standing there until the gate didn't open. He had to open it for her.

She let out a dismissive, "Oh. Thanks," and rushed over to the open cage.

He climbed the steps slowly and when they were seated inside, made sure their seatbelts were fastened. Then he locked up the cage and went down to the ride controls. As he pressed the button to start the ride, the girl let out a shriek of excitement and rattled the cage.

It was a shame. They were too perfect, but it was not time yet. He'd have to let this one go. For now.

CHAPTER FIFTEEN

It was after three in the afternoon. Mia sat in the front seat of her car, picking through a fruit salad she'd gotten at a local convenience store, since she couldn't take any more grease. This wasn't much healthier. The cantaloupe was a sickly yellow, the honeydew was mushy, and the grapes were bruised, and everything tasted the same—slightly metallic. But at least it wasn't a burger.

Setting it down, she looked around. She'd driven down a dirt road, and now she sat, overlooking a lake and thinking about what Smitty and Kiki had said about the carnivals that had passed through the area.

She'd never liked traveling carnivals like that. The rides were always rickety and in poor repair, and the operators always seemed a little shady. Nevertheless, whenever one came to town and Kelsey begged, Mia usually wound up being suckered into spending a night—and a lot of money—on creaky rides, impossible-to-win games, and terrible hot dogs.

Grabbing her burner phone, she looked up the non-emergency phone number for Dallas Fire Department and put in the call. A woman answered on the first ring. "Dallas Fire Department."

"Hello," she said. "I was wondering if you could help me. The fire department was responsible for that carnival last week, is that correct?"

"That's right. But it's over until next year."

"That's okay. I was there on the last day, and silly me, I left my purse on one of the rides," she lied. "I went back the next day but the carnival had been dismantled."

"I'm sorry to hear that. Have you tried the lost and found?"

"Yes, I did. No luck," she said scraping her top teeth over her bottom lip. "I was hoping that I could contact the carnival company you used, to ask if they might still have it?"

"Oh, uh . . ." the woman said. Mia could hear her shuffling papers in the background. "I'm sorry. I didn't set that up, and I'm not sure who I could ask. If you'll leave your name and number with me, I can call you back?"

No way. Bad idea. "I'll try to find it some other way. Thanks for your help."

She ended the call and searched for the number of city hall in Canton. Dialing that number, she drummed her fingers on the console as a voice said, "Canton Town Hall, how can I direct your call?"

"Hi. I'm looking for information about a carnival that took place a couple weeks ago in—"

"One moment," the voice said in monotone, and then she was filtered into a queue with a horrible Muzak version of The Police's "Every Breath You Take."

She waited, and waited, meanwhile, sweating away in the hot sun. She twisted the AC up to Max. The old beater car she'd gotten off a lot in the middle of nowhere didn't have the best air conditioning, and now, it seemed to be groaning under the demand. The last thing she needed was to kill her car. She decided to turn the AC down and bake.

After about ten minutes, a voice came on. "I'm sorry. Who are you holding for?"

"I'm looking for information about a carnival that—"

"Right. I remember. One moment."

Now, a Muzak version of Peter Gabriel's "Shock the Monkey."

Mia groaned and ended the call. There had to be a better way.

Yeah, Mia, there is a better way. If you were smart, you'd just go off far away and hide out. Or go back to Dallas and see if David's found anything new for you to use. You don't need to be wasting your time on other cases when your life is hanging in the balance like this.

For a minute, she almost gave up. She almost drove back to Dallas.

But then she thought of Linda, and how awful she'd looked. Her poor son. The whole poor family would never be the same. She couldn't give up now.

Sighing, she opened her browser and looked up the Dallas Fire Department. Sure enough, there was an advertisement for "FAMILY FUN at the FIRE DEPARTMENT CARNIVAL!" in bright yellow, with a big top and a clown. "Rides! Games! Entertainment! Food!" it said. "All Weekend Long!"

She scanned to the bottom of the advertisement. On the very bottom, there was a small line of type that said, *Presented by FunTime Amusements.*

Bingo. Excited, she went to the Canton Town Hall webpage and found a different advertisement for the "CANTON FAMILY CARNIVAL! ONE WEEK ONLY."

Underneath, it said, *Brought to you in conjunction with FunTime Amusements.*

All the air left her lungs. This was it. She was sure of it. The connection she was looking for.

Her fingers trembled as she looked for the next piece of the puzzle. She went to the search bar and typed in: *FunTime Amusements.*

It turned out, there were quite a few amusement companies under that name, so she clarified: *FunTime Amusements Dallas Canton.*

This time, the result she was looking for came up first. She clicked on the website and a site with balloons and big tops appeared. It said, *FunTime Amusements . . . We Provide the Fun!*

She scrolled down the page of offerings and stopped when she came to what she'd been looking for: *SPRING SCHEDULE.*

She paged down the list and saw Canton Town Fair. Right after that, Dallas Fire Department Carnival.

It could easily have been a coincidence. After all, there were thousands of carnivals, all over the country. Just because two couples died recently didn't mean there was a carnival serial killer, targeting couples.

She scanned up this list, to the names of the other towns the carnival had visited earlier. Texarkana. Fort Smith. Oklahoma City. Wichita Falls. One by one, she plugged the town names into the search bar, along with *Carnival* and *homicide.*

At first, she came up with very little. But then, she noticed a double-murder in a place called Pleasant Valley, outside of Wichita Falls. She read the article with interest:

TWO TEENS FOUND DEAD IN APPARENT MURDER-SUICIDE IN PLEASANT VALLEY

Wichita Falls, TX – Two people were found dead late Monday in the Park Middle School baseball field in the Pleasant Valley section of town in what deputies say appears to be a double murder-suicide.

The sound of shots fired was reported to the police department just before 10 p.m. on Saturday night, but the sheriff's department investigated and determined the sound heard was likely from a fireworks display at the local Cornhuskers Carnival, being held that weekend at the nearby Pleasant Valley Fairgrounds, adjacent to the Middle School.

According to the Pleasant Valley Sheriff's Office, the couple was found Monday morning by children attending baseball practice. Deputies arrived shortly after and found two people dead. Officials said one appeared to be victim of homicide and the other suffered a fatal self-inflicted gunshot wound.

Sheriff's officials said, "an investigation indicates that there is no danger to the public as we're nearly a hundred percent sure that this was a murder-suicide. It's an unfortunate occurrence and our hearts go out to the families of the victims."

The sheriff's office said that the victims died Saturday night. They were last seen by the victims' parents, who said they were attending a varsity football game at Pleasant Valley High School, which is about a mile from the baseball field where the bodies were found. According to the sheriff's officials, the two victims were students there.

No other details, including the identity of the victims, have been released.

Terri Maxwell, who attends Pleasant Valley High School, said she was friends with the victims who were killed Saturday night.

"They were very sweet people," Maxwell said. "Just a big loss. They knew a lot of people, you know, and they were a really popular couple. I can't believe that this happened."

Maxine Lakewood, who lives nearby, learned about the news when she woke up Tuesday morning.

"It's horrible. The news has rocked our town to the core. Pleasant Valley is a safe place. When you think of something like this happening, to two people who had their lives ahead of them, it's so sad."

Mia looked up from the screen, thinking. Then, out of curiosity, she typed in: *Texas – Murder- Carnival.*

She found a lot of results for the three murders she was aware of. But then she found another one, in Abilene, earlier that year. The headline read: *No Suspects in Murders of Local Teens.* She clicked on it and found that the Prairie Days Fair had happened there, just a few days prior to the murder.

Then she went to *FunTime Amusements'* webpage again. Sure enough, they'd been at the Prairie Days Fair, earlier that year.

With that, all the pieces seemed to click into place. Now, she was sure that her intuition was right. There were too many connections now for this to be a mere coincidence.

Whoever this killer is, he's following the list of carnivals. This was big news. Important news. Something the police or FBI should be warned about.

If only she could do something with the information. But what?

She went to the contact form on the Dallas Police page, to leave an anonymous tip. But one little mistake could bring down everything she'd done to keep herself away from the police. She didn't feel safe enough to have any contact with them, even through an anonymous contact form. What if they could somehow track her? And the local cops had been so quick to call these crimes murder-suicides. They probably wouldn't even pay attention to a tip. The FBI might, but then again, they got millions of anonymous tips. They would likely just sweep it under the rug.

Or even worse, they'd take it seriously and show up en masse, scaring the killer into hiding. They weren't exactly subtle when they decided to take a threat seriously. And if they did that, he might disappear into the woodwork, forever.

Her lips twisted as she thought about how to give the information to the authorities. She couldn't use David or Francine or anyone she knew as a middle-man—they were strictly off-limits. And if she tried to leave a note for David at their drop-off spot, he likely wouldn't get it in time to mobilize the FBI. They needed to act now.

She grabbed her fruit cup and tried to eat a little more of it, but it tasted even worse, now that it'd been baking in the heat for a half hour.

As much as she wanted to stick within striking distance of Dallas so that she could check on David's progress, she couldn't simply turn away from this information. If a killer was on the loose, chasing the carnival, something had to be done. The next place on the schedule was the Mansfield 4H Club Carnival in Mansfield, Louisiana.

Louisiana. She wasn't sure where Mansfield was, but it was likely hours away.

She checked the date up against the date on her phone. The 4H Club Carnival was starting today.

And maybe tonight, an unsuspecting young couple would go out for a night of fun, just like those other couples had . . . and die.

She punched the address of the carnival into her GPS. Mansfield was nearly three hours away. The clock on her dashboard read 3:35. If she left now, she would get there before the evening, before the carnival really got into full swing.

She wasn't sure who she was looking for. But it was worth a shot, if she could prevent another couple from being killed.

The joys of driving in rush hour, she thought, shifting her car into drive. She pulled out onto the road, heading east, toward Louisiana, on the hunt for a killer.

CHAPTER SIXTEEN

At a little bit after seven, Mia crossed the border into Louisiana. Traffic and her terrible AC meant that she was hot and uncomfortable, her clothes sticking to her skin with sweat. The hot breeze from the open window did little to help cool her down.

At least here, the entire state isn't looking for me, she thought, though it didn't give her much comfort. The FBI might have been looking for her here, too. She couldn't trust anyone.

As she crested a hill, her car started making an odd, banging noise, under the hood. She glanced at her GPS and frowned. She had about twenty miles to go before she reached Mansfield, and the way her old, suffering jalopy sounded, she wasn't sure it'd survive that long.

She turned off the vent, hoping that would give it a break. A breakdown right now was the last thing she needed. Not only would it leave her without a method of escape, but, though her pockets were pretty flush with money from David and Francine, she didn't have enough for repairs. And she needed that money for hotel rooms and food.

Probably serves me right for trying to push eighty. She pulled her foot off the gas and patted the dashboard. "Calm down, baby," she whispered to it, trying to coax it to behave. "You're all right. Let's just get to Mansfield and then you can rest."

It seemed to clank harder, as if some gears under the hood were grinding together. After another minute, a thin wisp of smoke appeared from the hood.

"Great," she said aloud. "It's overheating. Just what I need."

An exit was coming up. She pulled into the right lane and took the exit, cursing herself. The carnival was probably already underway, and the sun was beginning to set. In another few hours, it'd be a perfect time for that killer to strike. And she wouldn't be there.

Sighing, she took the ramp to a light and looked around for a service station. The best thing she could find was a dumpy old gas station that had only a couple of old-style pumps. But there was a garage there, even though it looked like it was closed. Maybe someone there could help her. She wasn't an expert on cars, but maybe it was something simple. Maybe all she needed was some water in the radiator, and she could be on her way.

The light at the end of the ramp was yellow as she made her way to it, but she didn't want to stop, because the clanking was even louder now, and she was afraid the car wouldn't start up again if she let it idle. As the light turned red, she rolled through and made the right turn.

"Come on, baby, just a little farther," she said to it, petting the steering wheel. "You can make it."

But then she heard the siren behind her. She looked in the rear-view mirror and saw the flashing blue and red lights, and her heart jumped in her throat.

Oh, no.

She slowed down and pulled to the side slightly, hoping he would just pass her by. Instead, he stayed on her tail. She moved to the curb and stepped on the brakes, her heart beating fast.

Shifting into Park, she looked around helplessly. *This isn't good. This isn't good. This is really bad!*

Her eyes caught on the burly cop with the moustache and mirrored sunglasses, still sitting in the front seat of his police cruiser. He was taking his time, a routine, leisurely stop. He hadn't pulled out his gun and aimed it at her. That was a good sign. Maybe he didn't know she was a wanted criminal.

Yet. He would know, eventually, if he tried to ask her for her license and registration, neither of which she had.

Calm down, Mia. Maybe he's just pulling you over to help you with your car. It was smoking up a storm now, so much so that she could barely see the gas station up ahead, even though it wasn't far away.

But his mouth was a straight line, showing he meant business. He reached for something under the dashboard and opened the door, then came sauntering toward her, holding his citation book in his hand.

Sweating hands still wrapped around the steering wheel, she stared straight ahead, trying to calm herself. The road ahead was clear. For a second, she imagined throwing the car into drive and tearing off, but a police chase? Really? She might have been a fugitive, but she couldn't bring herself to do that. Besides, she probably wouldn't make it a block, in the state her car was in.

When the officer reached her window and tapped on it, she realized she'd forgotten to roll it down. She grabbed the handle and cranked it, then managed a smile. “Hello, sir,” she said awkwardly. “Is there a problem?”

“Yes, yes there is. Ma’am, you know why I pulled you over?” he said in a heavy Southern drawl.

She bit the inside of her cheek, so hard she could taste the blood. “No, sir. I don’t.”

“You went through that red light back there.”

She looked over her shoulder. “I did? I thought it was yellow when I was going through.”

He shook his head. “I was waiting at the light when you went into the intersection. Caught the whole thing on my dash cam. So if you’re thinking you’re going to argue your way out of this one, you’re going to have some trouble.” He motioned with his hand. “License and registration.”

“Oh,” she said, reaching into the glove compartment. When she pulled it open, she found an old car manual she hadn’t known was in there. Nothing else. “Oh . . . it seems I forgot those things at home.”

He frowned and dipped his sunglasses, fixing his watery blue eyes on her. “You did?”

She nodded.

“I’m going to have to issue you a citation for that, Ms . . . what’s your name?”

“Donna,” she blurted, surprised at how fast the name came to her mind. “Donna Planderson.”

“Ms. Planderson. You came over from Texas? What’s your purpose?”

Her chest was starting to hurt from the pressure on it. She felt a bead of sweat slither its way down her ribcage. “I was just out for a drive.”

He let out a deep breath of air. “All right. Stay put here while I run your plates.”

She clenched her teeth hard. This would definitely not be good. But the car was smoking up a storm. She was as good as captured. When he walked away, she leaned her head against the side of the door frame and closed her eyes.

This is it.

For some reason, the dread deep within her mixed with another feeling. Relief. Maybe tonight, in prison, she’d get the first good night’s sleep she’d had in six months.

But no. If she let herself be captured, if her escape ended here, she'd never be able to give Wilson Andrews his comeuppance. And even worse, she'd never get home.

She had to play it cool. For as long as it took.

Mia watched the officer working in the car, stopping every so often to speak into his radio. Meanwhile, she shifted uncomfortably, imagining just what would happen if she went back to prison. She'd actually been in a maximum security women's institution for a few months, before the trial, and every day had felt like a lifetime. Back then, she'd kept telling herself that all she had to do was wait for the trial, where the jury would find her innocent, because she was, and the nightmare would end.

But now, if she went back? She'd live the nightmare, inside that cold, bleak cell, for the rest of her life. There would be no escape, ever again.

She'd never go home to Aiden or Kelsey, and their lives would be ruined as well.

At that thought, all the air left her lungs and a sharp stab of pain hit her in the chest. She brought a hand to her chest to calm her beating heart, just as the officer pushed open his door, stepped out, and walked toward her. This time, he wasn't holding anything, but his hand was firmly planted on the butt of his gun.

Oh, no.

"Ms. Planderson, would you please step out of the car?"

She looked up, affecting an innocent expression. "Is there a problem, officer?"

He nodded. "Yes, ma'am. A very serious one. This car was reported stolen in the Bracketville, Texas area, about a month ago."

She blinked. "Oh, is that right? I'm sorry, I didn't know. I borrowed the car from—"

"From whom?" He pulled off his sunglasses and stared at her.

"My neighbor," she said lamely. "I don't know her name. I was just--"

"Taking a drive, across state lines." He shook his head and reached for the door handle. "I think there's more to it than that. You'd better step out of the car."

The fight or flight instinct warred within her, but neither option was possible, now. She was caught.

With no other choice, she did as she was told. She knew the drill, but she played dumb and acted like this was her first time in an arrest situation. When he ordered her to turn around and put her hands on the top of the car, she felt the metallic fruit she'd eaten a few hours ago, fighting its way back up her esophagus.

He snapped the cuffs on her and said, "I'm sorry about this ma'am, but I'm going to have to take you in. We'll get this sorted out downtown."

Before she knew what was happening, he'd snapped a photo of her with his cell phone. She shrunk back, her heart beating like a drum inside her. Then he guided her toward the patrol car.

He began to read her the rights she knew by heart. This was worse than bad. This was *devastating*.. They'd *more* than get it sorted out downtown—they'd ask questions she couldn't answer without giving herself away. That U.S, Marshal was on her case, and he didn't miss a trick. If they put her mugshot in the system, it was only a matter of time before they discovered who she was. And then any chance of finding freedom would be gone.

CHAPTER SEVENTEEN

"Yes, Dana," U.S. Marshal Kane Wilcox said to his wife as he drove east of Dallas, to a place called Canton. "It's all good. I have been."

"Are you sure? You never take care of yourself, babe. You're always go go go, and you forget the important things. That was fine when you were twenty-five. But you're not getting any younger. And you know what the doctor said. You know how your blood sugar gets when you don't eat well," she said.

He could just see her, sitting in her garden. Though she kept busy with her activities, her main activity was worrying about him, even from several hundred miles away.

"I am taking care of myself, Dear," he said with a smile as he neared the Canton Gas 'n'Go. "And I have a little alarm on my phone reminding me to take the blood pressure pills. You don't have to keep reminding me. And you don't have to worry."

"I do worry! Eat something. I bet you haven't eaten all day. You're always on the move, chasing after these criminals, and you forget to eat."

Guilty as charged. He hadn't actually eaten . . . wow. Since lunch, yesterday? And that had just been an apple he'd gotten at a roadside stand.

No wonder he felt like shit.

He sighed as he pulled into the parking lot of the Horizon Motel. Their WANTED bulletins posted all over the internet were doing something, probably too well. Hundreds of calls were being phoned in every day, and it was up to him to check them out. Most of them were a waste of time. Some were pranks, called in by kids. Others were truly well-intentioned, but completely off-base. One person had sworn that they'd seen Mia, shopping at Target, and had actually detained her. The poor woman, who'd been shopping with her baby daughter, had looked nothing like Mia.

This time, someone had called in a sighting of Mia North at this motel, but had refused to leave a name. Though it would probably be just another dead end, it was his business to check it out. Probably another prank. The pranksters seemed to love drawing him out to the middle of nowhere.

Next to the motel was a little restaurant. When he spotted it, on cue, his stomach began to growl. As usual, Dana was right. He could probably use the pick-me-up. "Fine. I'll have something to eat. I'm here at the restaurant now, Dear. I'll speak with you later. Love you."

He ended the call and stepped out into the oppressive mid-afternoon heat, then made his way to the restaurant, dubiously eyeing the sign that said, *Tired of Fast Food? Try some of Momma's Flapjacks. Made with Love.*

No one can make flapjacks like Dana, he thought with a smile, remembering how she'd always make them in the shape of a heart, just for him. *But I'll give it a try, under her orders.*

He was used to stopping at greasy spoons, whenever he did remember to stop. But inside, to his surprise, he found something more his wife's speed. It was a place decorated like a gingerbread cottage, with Texas decor. A woman with a frilly apron and a bright smile greeted him, carafe of coffee at the ready. "Hi, darlin'. I'm Momma. Lunch for one?"

He nodded. She plucked a single menu from the hostess' stand, and as she led him to a spot with a red tablecloth, he reached into his pocket, pulling out Mia's mugshot, taken when she was first booked in, nearly six months earlier. According to reports, she hadn't changed her appearance much. As Momma set the menu in his lap, he held up the photo. "Seen her?"

She didn't look at the photo. "Are you police or something?"

He reached into his other pocket at pulled out his credentials. "U.S. Marshals."

"Oh." Her eyes widened and shifted to the photograph. The moment she met it, recognition sparked. "Why, yes. She ate breakfast here this morning. Although she only had a few bites of my legendary flapjacks. Seems to me like she was in a hurry to get somewhere."

He straightened. "This morning?"

She nodded. "Did she do something wrong? Why are you looking for her?"

He ignored the question. "Can you tell me what happened during your interaction?"

"Nothing, she just ordered breakfast, flapjacks, and I delivered them. That's all. She tipped well, but she didn't stay very long, like I said. Something lit a fire under her, and she took off," she said with a shrug. "I'm sure you have the wrong person. That girl was sweet as pie."

"So she was in a rush to get somewhere. Did she say where she was going?"

The woman shook her head. "No . . . " Her eyes lit up. "Oh, but now that you mention it, she was interested in the local area."

"Did you get the impression she was looking to put down roots here?"

"Oh, no. She was mostly concerned about the crime."

That was interesting. It made sense that Mia was digging into her own arrest, trying to find out evidence to save her own skin. "You mean, she was looking into a murder that happened in Dallas?"

"No. Oh, no. It was about something that happened around here." Her brow wrinkled. "In Canton."

Wilcox frowned. This woman seemed a little dotty. Did she have the wrong girl? Why on earth would a wanted criminal be pursuing trouble? Wouldn't they try to get away from it? But then again, Mia never ran from trouble. She seemed to like to be right in the thick of it. "Are you sure?"

She nodded. "Oh, actually, now, I remember it distinctly, honey. She was interested in the suicides that happened nearby. A couple of truckers were talking about it, and she was asking them questions about it."

This sounded more promising. He leaned forward. "What suicides were those?"

"Some kids. Police say they're suicides, but no one really knows. They were found dead by Two Acre Lake, not far from here. It was a real tragedy. But she thought the deaths seemed similar to others, if I remember, correctly? I don't know." She shrugged. "It didn't make much sense to me. But she lit out of here pretty fast, like she had somewhere to go."

"Do you know where?"

She shook her head. "Sorry, darlin'. She got in her car and headed toward that Two Acres Lake Park a few hours ago, and that was the last I've seen of her." She pointed at his menu. "You take a look at that and let me know what you want. Coffee?"

He shook his head and handed the menu back to her. "Sorry. I need to go."

Dana wouldn't be happy with him, but he couldn't help it. This couldn't wait. He squeezed past Momma and headed for the door, as something hit him. "You know what kind of car she was driving?"

She spun with the coffee carafe in her hand, and her brow tented. "Old. Dark blue. Small. Kind of looked like one of them clown cars to me. I'm not good with cars, honey, so I couldn't tell you."

He gave her the thumbs up, then stepped outside to his car. When he pulled out and headed east, he saw the sign for Two Acres Lake, and punched on the gas. This could be it. She was close. He could feel it.

But a moment later, when he pulled into the gravel lot, his spirits deflated. The lot was empty. He powered down the window, looking for any sign of life. There wasn't a single person on or around the lake. If Mia North had been here, she was gone, now.

He pounded the steering wheel with the heel of his hand. It was probably too much to hope that after all these weeks of searching, she'd just appear before his eyes, easy as that. No, Mia was a fighter, and she was smarter than that. She'd make sure he earned it, first.

Wilcox thought about what Momma had said. Something had brought her out to Canton, and he had a feeling it had little to do with her own escape. It was like being an FBI agent was in her blood, and she couldn't stop trying to solve mysteries, even if she wanted to. No, she was on the hunt for something. He was sure of it.

But what? He'd heard about the murder-suicide in Dallas. At Lookout Point. Was that what this was all about?

Grabbing ahold of his cell phone, he looked for any articles mentioning the case. When the first article came up, he clicked on it and read it over, thinking. Sure enough, the article mentioned that the police were looking into murder-suicide.

Lookout Point wasn't far from Mia's University Park neighborhood. There was a very real possibility that Mia North had a personal connection to that crime.

Then he looked up the Canton suicides, which had supposedly happened near Two Acre Lake, precisely where he was parked. As he read the article, he noted the similarities.

Two young couples, killed, one suspected to be a murder-suicide, the other, a suicide pact. Very interesting. Maybe she was looking for answers in those cases. But why? Wasn't she worried about saving her own skin?

It still didn't give him any hint as to where Mia North might have gone. And she wasn't here. She could be anywhere, now.

He leaned back in the seat of his car. This had been a waste of time. The sun was practically baking him alive, and he could feel the sweat soaking through his white, short-sleeved dress shirt.

He was about to shift the car into reverse and go back to that restaurant, to fulfill his promise to Dana to get something to eat when his phone started to ring. It was headquarters.

Damn. They're probably wondering why I haven't checked in today.

The reason was simple. He hadn't gotten anywhere. He thought he'd been on the right track when he came back up here from Bracketville. But now, he wasn't so sure. Yes, great, he'd been right—she had come back up toward Dallas. But other than that—he had little to go on. He didn't want to check in without having some solid evidence. The fact that Mia had likely been in Canton was a good start, but where had it led? Nowhere. Another dead end.

"Yeah?"

"Wilcox?"

That was a surprise. He'd been expecting his agent in charge. But it was Max Costa, a junior agent. His ears pricked up. Wilcox had it arranged so that any police activity involving someone matching Mia's description came straight to Max first, who'd relay it to him. "What do you got for me?"

"You told me to call if I came across anything in the Mia North case," he said quickly. "I think I got something."

He leaned over the steering wheel, anxious. "Yeah? What?"

"The police across state lines picked up a woman in a stolen vehicle. She hasn't been processed, but she fits Mia North's description."

"That right?" He started his car. "Across state lines?"

"Yep. Louisiana."

This was looking good. The border of Louisiana was a few hours away. If that was Mia, where was she headed now? "You have a make and model on that stolen vehicle? Color?"

"Looks like a Ford Festiva. Dark blue."

Bingo. "Where'd you say she was?"

"In Louisiana. The state police sent over a photograph."

Hell. It wasn't close by. But it didn't matter. He'd drive ninety the whole way, if he had to. "All right. Call them and find out where they're taking her, and tell them I'm on my way. Under no circumstances should they release her. Get the information and send it to me when you have it. Got it?"

"Will do."

He ended the call and sped out onto the highway. Dana wouldn't be happy with him. Not now, at least. But if he could put an end to this case tonight and come home to her tomorrow, she'd probably forgive him.

CHAPTER EIGHTEEN

Mia sat in the back of the police cruiser, her body adhering to the vinyl seats with sweat. The officer had the air conditioner blasting, but it wasn't helping at all.

I'm so screwed, she thought as she held her cuffed hands in her lap and stared out across the highway. Meanwhile, the officer was taking his time, sitting in front of her, filling out some paperwork. It was almost as if he wanted to prolong her misery.

She could just see it now—arriving to police headquarters, where the feds, including that U.S. Marshal Kane Wilcox, were waiting smugly, ready to take her into custody. Her name and likeness would be plastered all over national news, causing even more grief for her family.

At the thought, her eyes pricked with tears, but she blinked them back.

No, Mia. Think. You've got to get yourself out of this. You can do it.

Gnawing on the inside of her cheek, she analyzed her options. The officer was a little careless, yes, and seemed to be a good man with a soft spot. She had to think of a way out that wouldn't hurt him too badly, which narrowed her options. Killing an officer wouldn't help her case. She was desperate, but not desperate enough to risk another person's life to escape.

She leaned forward in the seat, so she was close to the cage separating her from the officer. "Excuse me," she said politely. "Is this going to take much longer?"

He grunted, not looking up from his paperwork. "It'll take as long as it takes."

She looked around. She had to do something, and quickly. Use the *I've got to go to the bathroom* ploy? No, that one had been used a thousand times. He'd be onto her. If she wanted to get free of these handcuffs, she had to think outside the box.

Mia spotted a bee, tapping its body up against the glass of the window nearest her. After a moment, it came to rest on the lip of the window, which was open an inch. Great. Bees loved her. They also loved stinging her, for doing nothing wrong.

Don't come in here, she thought silently staring up at the insect. *The last thing I want to do is be stung.*

At least she wasn't allergic. There was a boy in Kelsey's class that had been so allergic, he had to carry an epi-pen everywhere and went into hysterics, every time a bee even flew past their classroom window at school.

Suddenly, she had an idea.

She leaned forward again. "Officer, there's a bee in here," she said.

"Hmm," he said, disinterested. "What do you want me to do about it?"

"I'm allergic to bees. If I get stung, my throat closes up. It's really bad. I could die." She watched as the bee took flight in the cabin of the car, buzzing harmlessly toward the overhead light. "Look!"

The officer glanced in the rearview mirror, tilting his head, and must've finally seen the bee, because he said, "All right, relax," and moved to get out of the car. She bounced up and down on the seat, feigning alarm.

As he reached for his door handle and stepped outside, the bee bumped its way along the ceiling of the vehicle, finally reaching the window opposite and disappearing.

When the officer reached for her door, she sprung into action. "Oh, God, it stung me! It stung me!"

The officer leaned in. "Where?"

Mia had gotten plenty of welts and bruises on her body over the weeks. She just had to pick one. She held up her cuffed hands. "Right here! On the top of my hand!"

He stared at it. "Shit. Okay. I think we have an epi-pen . . . somewhere . . . " He started looking around helplessly.

"You think? I *know* I have one. In the trunk of my car."

"It's not your car."

"Semantics. Are you going to let me get it?"

"I'll get it," he said, taking a step toward the car. "You wait here!"

"You won't know where it is! You won't get it in time!" she cried, bringing her hands up to her throat. "Oh, God, it's closing up. I can't—I can't breathe--"

She leaned forward, clutching at her neck and gasping for air.

He reversed direction and returned to her. "All right. What do I do? Tell me where it is."

"Help—" she began, gasping and motioning toward the car. "Help me . . . over there. . . ."

He slipped an arm behind her back and helped her toward the car's trunk, then fumbled with the keys. She grabbed at them with her cuffed hands. "Let me . . ." she whispered in a weak voice, leaning on the car's trunk. She grabbed the keys to the car and attempted to open it, but dropped them. He fished them from the ground and handed them back to her, but it happened again. Shaking her head, she held out her hands. "Please . . . I need . . ."

"Right," he said frantically, realizing what she was asking, he found the keys to the handcuffs and made quick work of unlocking them. Her body slumped, limp, against the trunk, and he held her steady as her head lolled. "I got it. Miss, are you going to be okay? Look at me! Miss!"

The second the cuffs fell loose, she brought both hands up, hard, hitting him squarely underneath his jaw. The impact was bone-crushing because she heard the crack, saw the officer stumbling back to the ground. He let out a moan and blinked up at her, several times, stunned, but did not move as she stood over him, her shadow blocking out the sun.

"I'm sorry," she whispered to him, bringing another blow down on the side of his temple, knocking him unconscious. His body fell slack and his head drooped.

When she was done, she sat back, taking deep breaths, trying to calm herself. *You're lucky, Mia. Maybe you should listen to David and keep your head down. Because that was too close a call.*

She looked around the side of the road, making sure no one else had witnessed what she'd done, then grabbed the keys to her car. She thought about taking the officer's gun, but then decided against it. She didn't need to have anything else that they could trace.

Instead, she took the keys and went to her car. Every Louisiana state trooper would soon be crawling around, looking for it. She'd have to abandon it, soon.

She'd had some close calls before, but this was definitely the worst of them, the one that had made her entire life with her family flash before her eyes. She couldn't afford to do that again and jeopardize her chance at ever reuniting with her family.

And she wasn't out of the woods yet. The officer had snapped a photograph of her. So now, the police—and maybe the feds— would be breathing down her neck. Right now, she needed to get away from here, if only for a little while, until it was safe to come out again.

CHAPTER NINETEEN

An hour later, Mia pulled into the town limits of Mansfield, Louisiana, feeling like everyone in the world was watching her every move.

It was the car, she decided. She needed to lose it, and fast.

As she drove, she noticed the signs. *4H Club Carnival Food! Rides! Fun! June 4-7. JUST AHEAD AT THE FAIRGROUNDS! FIVE MILES!*

There was an old, abandoned gas station on the corner of the main drag, now a used car lot, with dozens of dusty old automobiles, parked along the perimeter. Someone had painted slogans on the front windshields of each car: *CLEAN! LOW MILEAGE! GAS-EFFICIENT!* She didn't notice anyone in the lot or in the main office as she pulled in.

Finding a spot beside the other cars, she pulled in, leaving the keys to the vehicle in the ignition. She didn't want to take the chance of trying to sell it and get money for it. Not now. It would severely limit her ability to buy another car, but right now, what was most important was that she put distance between herself and that vehicle.

Then she walked to the main road and stuck out her thumb. She didn't want to attract attention, but after the day she'd had, she didn't have the energy to walk five miles on her own. Plus, it was starting to get dark, and the carnival would be starting soon.

She'd been walking about half a mile, past a couple of fast-food restaurants, another gas station, and a post office, when a man in a rather new-looking pick-up truck stopped for her. Running to catch him, she peered in the window at an older man with a trimmed white beard. "Where you headed, darlin'?" he said.

"Just down the street, to the fairgrounds," she said.

"Aw, I'm going right past that. I live a little ways down there. I'll take you. Hop on in," he said, leaning over to pull his cowboy hat off the seat, so that she could sit.

"Thank you." She opened the door and pulled herself in, setting her backpack between her legs.

"Of course. Can't have a young girl like you out alone late at night. That wouldn't be gentlemanly of me," he said, checking his side mirror and pulling out onto the street. "Feel free to put that window up if it's no good for you."

"It's fine, thank you," she said, checking around to make sure no one was looking. She still couldn't shake the feeling that she was being watched. "So you live around here?"

He nodded. "All my life. So I can tell you're not from around here, huh?"

He was giving her a sideways glance, implying that she should tell him where she was from.

"You're right, I'm from Florida," she said quickly, dismissively. "Just hitching my way through this great country."

"Florida, eh?" He said it like he didn't believe her. Maybe he heard a little of her Texas accent, even though she never thought she'd had much of one, since most of the people in University Park weren't native and didn't have much of one, either. "Hitching? That could be dangerous for a little thing like you."

She shrugged. "I'm okay." *Change the subject, Mia.* "Can I ask you what might seem like a weird question? Has there been any news in the last few days? Regarding a young, teenage couple?"

He frowned. "What do you mean? What kind of news?"

"Maybe something that came out of that 4H Carnival?"

He shook his head. "I don't know nothing about that. They have contests there, and some kids win prizes for the best livestock, if that's what you mean?"

"No, it's all right. Forget it," she said. This town was small. If something had happened at this carnival, something told Mia that it would've rocked them all to the core. And yet, he didn't know about it. So that meant, either nothing had happened and she was way off base, or they hadn't found the bodies yet.

Either way, she had to check it out.

"Have you been to the carnival?" she asked, switching to a more pleasant line of questioning.

He nodded. "Brought my wife there on the first night. She bakes the best pies in the county. Won herself a blue ribbon, she did."

"Really? That's nice," she said as she stared out the window. With night falling, a delightful, cool breeze was now present, blowing through her hair. "I thought I would go and check it out."

"Oh." He frowned.

“What?” she asked, turning toward him. Maybe he’d just remembered some tragedy that had happened at the carnival.

“Well, I hate to be the one to tell you this, miss, but the carnival ended last night.”

She blinked. “It did?”

“Sure. It was only ‘til the seventh of the month.”

She gritted her teeth. That was one thing about constantly being on the run. She kept losing track of what day it was. She’d thought *today* was the seventh. “Today’s the eighth?”

He nodded and motioned out to a field. In the setting sun, she could just see a number of trucks carrying the rides, set up in a circle. One of them said *FUNTIME AMUSEMENTS.* A couple of plastic temporary fences were set up and there was a horse trailer parked in the mud. There were a few tents and a deflated big top, too, and the grass was scattered with the remains of carnival trash—streamers and popcorn tubs and soda cans. A half-deflated balloon trailed along the surface of the field, going wherever the wind took it.

“Oh, no,” she said as he pulled to the side of the road, by a bigger sign for the carnival.

He said, “I’m sorry, darlin’, that you’re missing out on all the fun. Can I take you to a hotel or somewhere else?”

She shook her head, wondering what she should do next. The carnival wasn’t happening now, but FunTime Amusements was still here, probably getting ready to move to the next place on the list. And that was what she’d come to look into. All was not lost.

“If you come home with me, I’m sure my wife will fix you something to eat,” he suggested.

She reached for the door handle. “Thank you, but I think I’ll just stay here,” she said, giving him a smile. “You’ve been very helpful. I appreciate it.”

He nodded, though his thick, bushy eyebrows tented together. “All right, miss, I hope you’ll be okay.”

“I will,” she said, slipping out of the truck, slamming the door, and hefting her bag on her shoulder. She waved at him as he pulled off into the distance.

She looked around. Other than the fairgrounds that the carnival had been set up on, there was no other sign of life. Trees, in all directions. *I really hope it is okay, here,* she thought, *because it probably is a really long walk to the nearest hotel.*

The walk to the barn and trailers was a long one, over a road that was deeply rutted by truck tires. The earth was dry, now, so she nearly tripped a few times over the uneven terrain. As she drew closer, she noticed a few tents set up next to the barn. A man with a black beard, in a dark leather vest and cowboy hat, came out of the barn. Looking around frantically, he caught sight of her and waved his hand.

"Hey. You. Come here and help me out."

She jogged closer. He pointed to the barn. "I got to take care of the horses." He reached into his pocket and pulled out a couple of keys. "Can you give these to Johnny so he can pull the truck around and load up the Tilt-a-Whirl?"

"Uh . . ." She looked around helplessly.

"Johnny." He clapped his hands sternly, clearly annoyed. "In tent three. Go."

Doing as he said, she jogged over to the tents, finding tent three among the series of five. It was easy enough, as all of them were marked. But then she stood outside, wondering if she was allowed to peek her head in. There was nothing to knock on.

Finally, she called, "Johnny?" and lifted the flaps.

She almost wished she hadn't. The first things she saw was a fat, naked man with a frighteningly hairy back, sitting on a cot, facing away from her.

As she was about to retreat, another man stepped forward. "I'm Johnny," he said, nudging her out of the tent. "You shouldn't be in here. No girls allowed. What's up?"

This man was attractive, maybe in his late twenties, with longish brown hair that reached his shoulders. He was fit, in a tight black t-shirt that hugged his frame and bulging biceps, and ripped jeans. He gazed at her, expectant, and it made her flush. "Who are you?"

"Oh." She held up the keys. "A guy—I don't know who he was—he wanted you to pull the truck around and work on the Tilt-a-Whirl?"

Johnny muttered a curse and shook his head. "Now? Jesus. It's almost dark." He looked around. "Guess it makes sense. We're way behind. Should've been out of here this afternoon. It's gonna make Many a bear to get set up by the weekend."

Many? What is he talking about? she wondered, but didn't ask. She'd already made enough of a fool of herself.

He started to stalk off, then turned.

"Hey. You want to help? I could use a hand."

"Sure," she said, rushing to catch up with him.

She followed him to a pick-up truck. He said, "I'm just going to back this right up to the ride over there. You make sure I don't hit anything, okay?"

Mia did as she was told, watching as he backed the truck toward the ride, and motioning for him to stop when it was time. He hopped out and said, "So, you don't know Buck. Something tells me you're not on our payroll?"

She shook her head slowly. "No. I don't even know who—"

"Wanna be?"

"What? I—"

"Buck—the guy with the beard— owns FunTime. But I'm the brains of the operation." He reached out a hand for her to shake. "Johnny Rose. And you are?"

"Rolanda," she said, saying the first name that popped into her head as she shook his hand.

"Rolanda?" He shook her hand slowly, appraising her. For a moment, she thought he might be onto her. But then he said, "You here looking for a job? We're always hiring carnies. Whenever we go on the road, most of our people tend to run off when they find something better. We're hurting. We lost ten guys in Texas."

"Ten?" she asked, wondering if it had anything to do with the murders. "Why?"

He shrugged. "Just normal attrition."

"Ten! That's a lot. How many guys work for you?"

"More than a hundred. On and off. Like I said, we lose people over the course of the season. Usually not this many, but we pick new people up all the time."

A hundred. That was a lot. Was one of them a killer? Was the killer one who'd fled the carnival, and that was why they hadn't struck here in Mansfield? Or maybe the killer was just laying low, like she was. Maybe he was here right now.

Maybe she was talking to him right now.

She shivered at the thought and hugged herself tightly. "What would I be doing?"

"Same thing us guys do. We're not going to have you doing nothin' you can't handle, don't worry about that. Operating rides, setting up food stations, filling in wherever you're needed. It's important to be flexible." He winked. "We all help each other around here."

Johnny didn't seem like a serial killer. He was a little smarmy, a little slick, but he wasn't the typical weird, antisocial misanthrope, who neighbors always said on news reports, afterwards, *Quiet, kept to himself.* "And the pay?"

"Pay's pretty good; it's under the table. And we don't care what kind of baggage you brought with you, so don't bother telling us. But I'm warning you. You're gonna be hustling. We got plenty to do while the carnival's in town, and we're always moving. So are you in?"

She paused, mulling it over. Well, if there was one way to stay anonymous, this was it. She could travel along with the carnival as her cover. It was actually perfect.

Not to mention that if the killer of those young couples was a part of this traveling carnival, she might be able to get close enough to weed out who he was.

"Sure. I'm in."

"Good." He nodded. "Let me just get done with this, then I'll find Shirley and she can get you set up with a cot for tonight in the women's tent. Okay?"

"You don't have to go looking for me, honey," a voice said. Mia turned to see a woman wearing a tight, cleavage-baring gingham-check tank-top and painted-on short-shorts. She had fire-red braids that touched her shoulders and a bright smile, outlined in bright-red lipstick. Stepping forward, she appraised Mia, too. "Hi. New blood?"

Johnny grinned at her. "Yeah, baby. Shirley, this is Rolanda. She's our new girl. Can you get her set up in the tent, show her around?"

Shirley nodded. "Of course. Come on, girl." She looped her arm through Mia's. "Where you all from? And why you out traveling so late?"

"Florida," she said, since she'd already used the lie before. "Just got into town and I'm looking for work."

"Well, you found it. Not that it's very good. It actually kind of sucks, because Buck will work you 'til you die," she said with a laugh. "But they don't ask questions. And I like that. Plus, you meet all kinds of people and get to see the country. I've been all over the South in the year I've been with Buck."

She led her to another big tent, next to tent three, and pushed aside the flap. When she did, a shaft of light shone on Shirley's face, showing crow's feet around her eyes. Before, Mia would've placed her at late twenties, but now, she saw that she was much older, maybe mid-forties. "Welcome to the fray," she said with a laugh.

Mia stepped inside to find two rows of cots, and women of all sizes, ages, and colors, sitting among them, some talking, some dancing to soft music that played on the radio, some painting their nails. Most didn't look up when she appeared, but an older woman with a short, boyish haircut shouted, "Oh, no, Shirley, you suckered in another one?"

Shirley patted Mia on the back. "Rolanda, this is Bertie, our house manager. She makes sure all of us have everything we need. Bertie, Rolanda's our new recruit."

Bertie pulled her legs up under her on the cot. "Well, you're just in time for our drive to Many."

"Many?" Mia asked.

"Yeah, another town down in East Nowhere, Louisiana. Where it'll be even hotter than it is here," she said, motioning to the cot next to her. "You can sleep here. Unless you're hungry? There's probably some cold chili left in the mess hall, if you're interested."

Shirley made a scared face. "Bo's chili isn't good when it's hot. We don't want to scare her away."

Bo. Maybe he was the killer. She doubted the killer was a female, based on her knowledge of serial killers, but maybe Bo would provide some information. "I could eat."

Shirley took her bag and threw it on the cot. "In that case, come right this way. But don't say I didn't warn you, Ro."

Mia followed her out of the tent, half-expecting to find the police there, having caught up with her after that last misstep. Luckily, they were alone in the vast field. Shirley brought her to the next tent over, where a thick smell of cumin and other spices assaulted her nostrils.

"One bowl of chili, and then it's lights out," Shirley said. "We've got to get on the road bright and early tomorrow morning."

Mia nodded. Looking for a killer while traveling anonymously, as far away from the police as possible? Yes, that would be a very good thing.

CHAPTER TWENTY

Kane Wilcox crossed the border into Mansfield at a little after eight in the evening. By the time he got down to the police station where the "car thief" was supposedly being held, it was after nine.

Judging from the size of the station—barely bigger than a one-room schoolhouse—Wilcox wagered there wasn't much happening in this corner of the state. Surprisingly, though, when he walked inside, the small station was in a flurry. A harried woman with short, brassy curls barely looked up as she fussed behind the front desk, a phone jammed between her cheek and shoulder.

Wilcox stood there for a good two minutes, waiting for her to acknowledge him as she shouted into the phone. "I know! Isn't it? It's absolutely the craziest thing I've ever heard. Poor him! Can you believe that? Yeah, a little woman! He's all shaken up, never had a woman hurt him like that before."

Wilcox rolled his eyes to the ceiling. He didn't have time to listen to small-town gossip.

Then she said, "Well, now she's on the run, the crazy lady. So lock your doors and bring your kids inside."

He narrowed his eyes. She wasn't talking about . . . could she be . . . ?

Mia North . . . escaped? Again.

Oh, shit.

He banged a fist on the counter. The woman looked up, alarmed. He flashed his badge.

She stopped her gossiping abruptly and said, "Honey, I've got to call you back." She placed the phone down in the cradle and said, "You're the Marshal they said they were sending over."

He placed both palms on the counter and leaned forward, craning his neck to see into the interrogation rooms beyond the reception area. "Where is Mia North? Is she here?"

The woman shook her head. "I don't know who Mia North is, but we're a little discombobulated." She looked over her shoulder into the office behind her, and shouted, "Bob! That U.S. Marshal is here!"

A man with a bald spot and a terrible beer gut stepped out of the office, hand extended. "Agent Wilcox?" he said as Kane shook his hand. "It's a real pleasure to have you here. I'm Chief of Police Robert Saunders. Why don't we step into my office?"

He shook his head. "I'd like to talk to the suspect in the car—"

"Why don't you come in here, first, and we'll discuss it?"

Reluctantly, Wilcox followed Saunders into his office, listening to him babble on about the call they'd received. "I tell you, it's not every day we get a call from the feds. We're pretty quiet around here. We don't have very much happening around these parts. So of course Anita patched it right through to our officer. And he had instructions to bring her right in to our humble headquarters here."

There was a half-eaten, pink-sprinkled donut near his computer, and a picture of him standing on a beach with a good-looking family of at least ten kids. Wilcox glanced at these things and lowered himself into a chair. "Is Mia North here?"

Saunders sat down and laced his fingers together. "She must've done something pretty bad, for you to be crossing state lines and going after her, huh?"

"There's a statewide manhunt going on for her in Texas. She's an escaped convict."

His eyes widened. "Geez. Is that right?"

Wilcox folded his arms over his chest. *Enough of this bullshit.* "Chief, let me see her. Now."

Saunders rubbed the back of his neck. "Well, it's a funny thing. I'd let you, but the thing is, she escaped."

"What? What the hell happened?"

The chief turned his palms upward, his face turning pink. "If we'd known—if someone had told us she was a dangerous criminal, we might've taken extra care. But our officer said she faked an allergic reaction. He didn't know what to do, so he took the cuffs off. She assaulted him, knocked him out, and took off in that stolen vehicle."

Wilcox clenched his fists in his lap. "Shit. When was this?"

"About two hours ago."

His mouth opened, and nothing came out. Two hours? She could be all the way across the state by now. He growled, "Why the hell did no one tell me this?"

Saunders shook his head. "I'm sorry, but if we knew—"

He waved the chief away. “She’s in the blue car, right? We have details on it? Does the officer have any idea where she might’ve been heading?”

The chief looked down at his lap. “We have all the details on the car she went off in, and we’ve put out an APB to find it. But as for where she was heading, she knocked him out cold. He woke up fifteen minutes later, and she was gone.”

“Great.” He stood up and stalked to the door. He’d been close. So close. And now, what did he have?

He pulled out his business card. “Call me directly if you come up with anything. Immediately, you understand?”

The chief glanced at the card and nodded.

He stepped out of the headquarters and strode to his car, thinking. By now, it was almost dark. Mia was no idiot. She likely knew he was on her case, so she wouldn’t stick around for very long. Knowing her, she’d probably set out with that car, gotten a safe distance away, and ditched it for another ride.

And she was on the hunt for something. So what had brought her out here in the first place? Was she on the trail of a murderer who’d been involved in the killings of those two young couples? If so, what detail had brought her all the way out to Mansfield? What made her think that the killer would strike all the way out here?

Chief Saunders words echoed in his head: *We don’t have very much happening around these parts.* He’d have mentioned if there’d been a murder or suicide of a young couple, wouldn’t he have? But there had been nothing. So what was Mia North chasing after?

He’d missed something. With these two cases, he’d clearly glossed over something that Mia North had caught. Something that tied them together.

Frowning, he pulled up the articles for the two cases and read them over, again and again, trying to see the similarities. Tomorrow, he’d go back and interview the people involved. He’d find that thread, tying the two cases together, and he’d pull it.

Because he was pretty sure, at the end of it, he’d find Mia North.

CHAPTER TWENTY ONE

As promised, the carnival was on the move, bright and early. Mia had been woken up from the soundest sleep she'd had in a while, to find that they were already pulling up the stakes of the tent she was sleeping under. She made it to the mess hall in time to eat a bowl of runny oatmeal—provided to her by Bo, a ninety-something year old man who could barely walk, much less climb a hill and murder two innocent young people—and then she was put to work, packing everything up for travel to a town called Many.

Now, she was in the back of a van with a couple of other carnies. They were at the tail end of a long caravan of trucks, stretching over to the next stop. There was Shirley, and Bertie, and a couple of men. There was Will, a kid who couldn't have been more than twenty, who was obsessively playing with a Rubik's cube, Frank, his father, who was driving, and then Randy, a large, slovenly young man who talked incessantly and punctuated everything he said with a loud, honking, "Haw!"

Mia didn't speak unless spoken to. Instead, she watched them all, trying to gauge whether or not any of them could have committed the murders of those couples.

She eliminated Shirley and Bertie, not simply because they were women, but because they seemed too normal and down-to-earth to do anything so cold. Randy, with his massive, lumbering frame, seemed a little too goofy, a little too outspoken to be a closet serial killer. Frank hadn't said much. The few times he spoke, he seemed to bark, but his appearance, with a clean polo, bald head and beer belly did give off normal dad vibes.

But Will? He was another story altogether. He slouched in his chair, his hood up, his face hidden from the rest of the van's occupants. Whenever his father asked him anything, he just grunted. Frank said that Will was taking a gap year for college, but when Mia asked him what he was looking to study, Will had only shrugged and said, "Don't know."

“Oh, come on, you have some ideas, boy. Tell them,” Frank demanded, looking at him through the rear-view mirror.

“Mind your own goddamn business,” he’d muttered back, turning away.

Mia couldn’t see his eyes, but she wasn’t sure she wanted to. All she saw was an acne-scarred chin, with a few stray whiskers, not nearly enough to be a full-grown man’s beard. He was shaking a little, too, which made her curious about him.

So she tried again, even though she’d been told to mind her own business. She’d never been very good at that, anyway. “Do you like working for the carnival, Will?” she asked.

He shrugged. “Got no choice.”

And that was that. But her suspicions were definitely aroused. Though she’d met dozens and dozens of carnies over the past few hours, young Will had quickly risen to the top of her list of suspects.

“Hey, guys, we’re here,” Bertie said from the front seat. “Many, Louisiana.”

Frank said, “Actually, it’s pronounced, *Ma-nee.*”

Bertie shrugged. “Whatever. Don’t look too bad. Where’s the fairgrounds?”

Frank looked around. “Just following the caravan, wherever they take us. It’s got to be around here somewhere.”

Mia looked out the window and saw a sign that said, “Welcome to Many, the Heart of Toledo Bend.” They entered a little shopping district that looked just like Main Street, USA. She watched houses and buildings, a little town hall, and a small department store pass by, and eventually, they were out in the country again. A moment later, they passed a sign that said, “Sabine Parish Fairgrounds.”

The van turned down a dirt road leading into the grassy field, bumping over the rutted land before coming to a stop behind the other vehicles.

Bertie clapped her hands. “Looks like we’re on! Move it, move it, move it,” she instructed like a drill sergeant.

Mia blinked and stretched, preparing to get out of the van.

Shirley rolled her eyes and looked at Mia. “She’s always like this, Rolanda. I don’t think Bertie has an off switch. If she has one, sometimes I wish someone would flip it!”

She climbed outside after Shirley. “So what are we expected to do?”

“Anything they tell you to,” she said with a shrug. “Last time I set up the snack stand and started getting the food ready. We’re in a time crunch for that. The carnival opens tonight at seven.”

“Tonight?” She looked around in shock. It seemed impossible that in just a few short hours, this empty field would be full of people, enjoying the rides and attractions. “Wow.”

“Come on,” Shirley said, tugging on her sleeve. “I’ll show you the food trailer. Old Bo’ll be there, and he always needs help.”

Mia followed her across the grounds, holding back slightly, because she was interested to see what Will was up to. Frank, his father, had him up against the side of the van and was wagging a finger at him, giving him a stern talking-to. About what, she wasn’t sure. He smacked him on the side of the head. “Get over there,” he growled, in a frighteningly evil voice that was the exact opposite of the one he used while driving the van.

Now, Mia couldn’t help looking at Frank. *Jekyll and Hyde, much?* With that temper, maybe she should’ve been looking at him.

“Hey.” Shirley snapped her fingers and Mia. “Ro. You coming?”

“Right, yes,” she said, tripping to keep up as she watched Will stalk over to where a bunch of men were setting up the fun slide.

When he was out of sight, she noticed the buzz of activity around her. Immediately, people had jumped into action, working to put the rides up and get everything ready for the night. They functioned like a well-oiled machine, knowing exactly what to do.

Mia had to admit, she was impressed; it looked as if this crew had set up many carnivals before. *And how many other murders were committed at them?* she wondered, making a mental note to look into other couple-deaths that had occurred near carnivals. Maybe there were even more.

Shirley stopped at a white fiberglass trailer with a fold-down side that had a window in it. She knocked on the door, and Bo called, “Come in!”

They stepped inside an impossibly small kitchen area. The truck itself was large, but the kitchen was so packed with equipment that there wasn’t much breathing room. Mia found herself wedged in a corner as Bo and another man ran around, moving back and forth between a large freezer and the giant grills.

“Come on, gals,” the man said. “We got to get all this stuff thawed out before opening time!”

"Okay, Greg," Shirley said, pointing to Mia. "Ro, this is Greg. He helps Bo out."

Greg had shaggy blonde hair and looked a little like a surfer, right down to the flower-print, open-necked Hawaiian shirt and flip-flops. "Nice to meet you, Ro. You new?"

Mia nodded.

"Yep, she got stuck here like the rest of us," Shirley said, reaching into the freezer and pulling out a sleeve of hot dogs.

Mia reached in and pulled out something that looked like hamburgers. "What's on the menu?"

"The standard," Greg said with a grin as he took the burgers from her. "Hot dogs, corn dogs, hamburgers, fries, funnel cakes, soft drinks, and gallons and gallons of lemonade. Your typical heart attack." He motioned with his chin toward a large box. "Grab that for me?"

She reached over and grabbed it, handing it to him. "Wow, how much of this stuff do you make?"

"Oh, we'll sell a thousand dogs tonight, I bet."

Her eyes widened. "And Bo and you cook all that?"

"Bo doesn't do so much of the cooking anymore. Just the serving. Hey." He smiled at her. "I'm looking for someone to help cook. What do you say?"

She hedged. Truthfully, she'd have rather been outside, walking around the grounds, so she could keep her eyes open. Stuck in the food truck, she wouldn't be able to keep an eye on things. "I'm not much of a cook. I've never made a funnel cake in my life."

"Don't worry. It's not rocket science. I'll show you all you need to know."

It looked like she couldn't get out of it. Maybe it wouldn't be so bad. They wouldn't keep her chained to the stove, would they? She could get out, take breaks, and observe.

She especially wanted to observe young Will, and now, Frank, who were working somewhere out there, out of her line of vision. But maybe, even if she couldn't see them, she could learn about them another way.

Shirley and Bo went to the back of the truck to work on grabbing the rolls for the burgers and dogs. As Greg showed her the process for frying the French fries, she said, "So how long have you been in this business?"

Greg wiped the sweat from his brow with the back of his hand. It was almost intolerably hot by the fryers. In fact, despite the loudly blowing fans, the entire truck felt like an oven. “I’ve been with Buck and FunTime for five years.”

“Oh, then you know everyone,” she said.

He nodded. “Yep, today, the only one I didn’t know was you.” He winked, and she stiffened, wondering if he was trying to come on to her. “Why do you ask?”

“Well,” she said, ignoring the comment and taking a step back so he wouldn’t think she was flirting. “We drove down here from Mansfield with a father and son. Frank and Will?”

Greg nodded. “Yep.”

“What do you know about them?”

He shrugged. “Good people. Frank works well. Will’s a typical teenager, but he’s growing. Give him a couple years.” He cocked his head at her. “Why do you ask?”

“No reason,” she said quickly, hoping her curiosity didn’t give her away. “He was just yelling at his son, and I worried there was some trouble there.”

“Nah. Frank’s got his head on straight. He’s former military. Can be intense. That’s all.”

“Oh, okay,” she said, looking down at the basked of fries in the hot oil. They were only supposed to be in the first basket for forty-five seconds, and as she stared at them, she realized she’d forgotten to time them. “Do I take these out now?”

He eyeballed them. “Yeah. Move them to the next vat.”

She did as she was told, feeling deflated. That hadn’t helped her find out much at all. Buck, the owner of it all, was a bit of a cowboy, but probably too busy to go around killing people. Johnny seemed like a good guy, a little wild, but not the killing type. Greg was the surfer, a bit of a flirt, but nothing awful. Will was sullen and removed, but he might’ve been a typical teenager. Frank could be hard-edged, but that might have been his military background. And then there was Bo, the old man, likely too frail to go around committing murders. And the women, Shirley and Bertie, and all the other carnies she hadn’t yet met . . .

Her mind reeled. She’d met so many people in such a short time, but there was nothing about any of them that stood out to her as a definite red flag. Soon, night would fall, and a killer might be on the loose.

The only question was, would she be able to find that killer before he struck again?

CHAPTER TWENTY TWO

Long before seven o'clock, the streets outside the fairgrounds began to fill with cars, and by opening, the gravel parking lot adjacent to it was full. Parents with their young children, couples, and groups of teenagers flocked to the fair, so that even before the sun went down, an enormous crowd had gathered.

From Mia's spot in the food truck, it looked almost like standing room only. She handed over a bag of cotton candy to an excited ten-year-old, took the cash in exchange, and stuck it in the register, then only managed a glance out at the throng of people before her next customer came up.

"Fries, please!" a teenage boy said.

"One moment," she said, spinning to fill a cup with fries. She'd started out with cooking, but then Greg had taken a break at the counter. Shirley had come back from her break, and was now trying to make a funnel cake for another customer.

"Fun, huh?" she said as Mia wavered on her feet, affected by the heat, the loud lilting music of the calliope, and the crowd.

"Yeah, great," she murmured, packing the fries in and salting them. She turned to give it to the customer, who handed over his money. She gave him his change. "Thanks. Have fun."

Finally, there was a break in the crowd. She fanned her face as she looked out of the window. It was dark, now, and the bright lights of the rides and attractions illuminated the night. From here, she could see the Ferris wheel spinning, the Frog Bog game, a Test Your Strength game, and the funhouse mirror pavilion. Kids ran from place to place, shrieking. Young couples strolled, hand-in-hand. Nothing looked amiss. It was just like any other carnival she'd ever been to.

"Fun times," Shirley said, slinking next to her.

"Yeah . . ." she said, realizing that she might be able to press Shirley for information. "But it can't be all fun. I'm sure you've seen your share of shady characters."

She snorted. "Oh, sure, I have."

"Even part of the carnival staff, too. Am I right?"

Shirley raised an eyebrow. “Of course.”

“So,” she said, turning to the woman. “Tell me! What’s the juiciest bit of gossip you have?”

She smirked. “Oh, get this. Ro, you’re not going to believe it.” She grabbed Mia’s hand. “The last stop we were at? In Mansfield? I was just going to the porta-potty, thinking everything was just fine. It said it was unoccupied, so I opened the door. And guess who I saw in there?”

“Who?” Mia asked, not sure if this was the kind of information she was digging for.

“Bertie. And Bo!” She smiled broadly. “Can you believe it? They were totally hooking up. And it’s crazy because he’s like, half-dead.”

“Oh,” Mia said, less than enthused. That definitely wasn’t the gossip she was hoping for. She decided to try again. “But I’m sure there’s some pretty dangerous people in the carnival crowd, too, right? Like, anyone you think might be a future serial killer? Like . . . uh, Will, for instance?”

Shirley snorted. “Uh, yeah . . . well, all of them, really, could be. Otherwise they’d get real jobs. Most of us are pretty sketchy, if you ask me. Have a few more skeletons than most. You, included.” Her smile faded. “But that’s the thing about carnies. We keep our histories to ourselves. We don’t take too kindly to people prying too much. So I wouldn’t ask too many questions, Ro.”

Mia bit her tongue. Yes, all these people were running from something. If she kept asking questions, she’d probably put a big target on her back. “I’ll keep that in mind.”

Another customer came to the window, a woman holding a toddler girl. Mia was about to help her, when Shirley said, “You haven’t taken your break yet. Why don’t you go?”

Mia wanted to. It was the only way she’d be able to properly scope the place out. But Greg still hadn’t come back. “Are you sure? I don’t want to leave you alone.”

“Greg’ll be back any moment,” Shirley said, waving her on. “I’ve got it under control.”

“Okay.” Mia took off her white apron and used it to wipe the sweat from her forehead. Then tossed it aside and stepped out the door, onto the carnival fairway.

She walked through crowds of people, enjoying the carnival, past the fun slide and the carousel, looking for anyone who appeared like they might be up to no good. When she reached the picnic area, a set of about ten wooden tables, assembled under a tent, someone grabbed her shoulder.

"Rolanda!" It was Buck, the owner of FunTime amusements.

"Oh, hi—" she said lightly, before she realized how cross he looked. "Is something wrong?"

He put his hands on his hips. "I'd say something's wrong. Look."

He pointed down at an overflowing garbage bin next to one of the tables.

"Yeah, well, I'm on break from working at the food tent, so—"

"You think I give a crap?" He scowled at her, his hands on his hips. "We're a team here. And that means that when you see something wrong, you fix it. Garbage duty. Now."

He seemed to notice something else awry, behind her, and ran off, likely to get in someone else's face. That left Mia with a pile of gross, foul-smelling garbage to take care of. As she was preparing to take the lid off and remove it, she noticed that there were several other overflowing bins, too. Apparently, no one else on the "team" cared enough to fix this particular problem.

And so much for my fifteen-minute break. Labor laws probably don't mean anything to these people.

Sighing, she removed the lid, shoved the used paper plates and lemonade cups into the bag, and lifted it from the bin. Inside, she found the roll of new bags. She opened one up, fixed it in place, and attached the lid. As she did, a kid came by and tossed a nearly-full drink in there, spraying her with lemonade.

She scowled at him, and as she was wiping off the front of her wet, sticky t-shirt, she happened to look across the fairway and notice a man with long, stringy dark hair, in an AC/DC t-shirt, leaning against a tent pole, watching people go by. But he wasn't just watching anyone go by.

He was watching a young woman in a yellow sundress, walking arm-in-arm with a preppy, college-type kid in cargo shorts and a polo shirt.

As she moved to the next garbage can, lugging the full trash bag with her, she couldn't take her eyes off him. He was sucking on the straw of a drink cup, watching their every move. When the couple stopped so the man could test his strength, the man's eyes followed. She watched closely, sure she'd seen him before. He was a carny, one of the people she'd seen setting up the rides, earlier in the day, but she'd never been introduced to him.

If he was one of the carnies, that meant he'd likely been in the other locations.

The college boy tried to pound the sledgehammer down so the bell would ring, but even after three tries, he still couldn't make it. The woman in the yellow sundress giggled, and after he came back to her, shrugging, arms raised in a *well-I-tried* gesture, she gave him a kiss on the cheek and they continued on their way, toward the other booths.

Still laughing together, he took her hand and led her behind the fortune teller booth, out of sight.

Mia shifted her gaze to the carny. He'd left his spot at the tent and was now striding purposefully after them.

Garbage duty forgotten, Mia skipped into a run after them. When she got to the booth of Madame Fortuna, the fortune teller, and looked behind it, there was no one there. This area, between the booths, was not a normal aisle for traffic, so it was empty. She stepped forward, into the row of booths, where the shadows cast her in darkness, looking up and down the rows, for the man, the couple. Where had they gone? Had he gotten to them so soon?

When she heard a muffled whimper, she ran to it, ducking between two booths, and . . . running right into the back of the carny. She only had a split second to gauge what was happening—the couple, standing frozen, eyes wide with shock, the carny, holding a blade that glistened in the moonlight—because in the next moment, he whirled, swiping the knife in an arc in front of her.

She managed to duck beneath the knife, then reach out, grabbing for the man's wrist. He moved out of the way at the last moment. Somewhere ahead, the girl screamed. Mia pivoted and brought her leg behind his as he stepped backwards, and he stumbled to the ground, dropping the knife.

Mia lunged for the knife, grabbing it before the man could, and knelt over it, bringing it to his throat. "Don't move."

He stared up at her, wide-eyed. "Okay," he said, trembling in fear.

Something was wrong. She'd expected a little more of a fight from a hardened serial killer. But this guy was giving in.

"Whoa," the college guy said, standing over them. "Where'd you come from? I was handling it."

His girlfriend rolled her eyes. "Sure you were. We were about to get all our money stolen."

Mia grabbed the guy by the front of his t-shirt, lifting him up. As she did, she noticed the man's wallet that had fallen underneath him. So that's what this was? A simple mugging?

"What were you doing?" she demanded of the carny, shaking him.

"I just—" He gave her a pathetic pout. "I just wanted some extra money to send back to my family."

"What about the other stops on the carnival? You know about the murders?"

"I do, yeah! But it wasn't me!" His body trembled. "I swear. I wasn't even in Dallas. I had to go home for my mom's funeral. Ask anyone."

Great. She'd caught a thief, but she'd also nearly blown her cover. And that wasn't something she could afford to do right now.

Standing up, she handed the college his wallet and the knife. "Keep him here. Call the police," she said, dusting off her jeans.

Then she ran off, hoping that no one would notice what she'd done. She couldn't keep doing that, getting in the middle of situations like that. The more she did, the more her cover would come off. And now, she had to admit, she was a little disheartened. The killer hadn't struck in Mansfield, at least, as far as she knew. And if he hadn't struck tonight, either . . . maybe he truly was gone? Maybe he'd never been part of the carnival in the first place, and she was barking up the wrong tree?

By the time she got back to the picnic pavilion, the garbage was cleaned up, and Buck was standing there, hands on hips. "There you are!" he growled at her. "Where did you go?"

She pointed behind her. "I—"

"You know what? I don't care," he muttered, taking her by the arm. "You're on clean-up duty tonight. I want this place absolutely free of any garbage after the last guest goes home. You understand?"

She nodded obediently, just happy that he hadn't noticed she was involved in the mugging incident. As he led her over to another overflowing trash can, police sirens blared in the distance, over the sound of the carousel's music.

They were quickly coming closer. Buck listened and muttered a curse, stomping his boot on the grass. "Dammit. What happened now?" He took a step in the direction of the sirens, but stopped and wagged a finger at her. "Remember. You don't get off tonight until the entire grounds are trash-free! You get it?"

"Yes, sir," she said, and watched him walk toward the police officers, who were just coming in out of the parking lot. All around, people were whispering of a possible mugging that might have taken place.

Keeping her head down, Mia grabbed the full trash bag, replaced it with a fresh one, and threw the trash in a dumpster at the rear of the fairgrounds. She checked all the other trash cans as she walked back to the food truck, noting how much scattered garbage was already all over the place. She hoped other people were going to be on the night crew with her, because otherwise, she'd never get to sleep.

At least there was no line at the food truck. The crowds appeared to be thinning out, the evening winding down. "What happened to you?" Shirley said when she finally stepped into the truck.

"Oh, Buck cornered me and had me do trash duty," she explained, glad she had a good cover for the mugging she'd intercepted.

"Really, ugh! Sorry about that," Shirley said as Mia put her apron back on. "Did you hear about the excitement?"

Mia feigned surprise. "What excitement?"

"Turns out Steve, one of the carnies, tried to mug someone. They arrested him! It was pretty exciting."

"Really? And I missed it," Mia said, shrugging. "Oh, well."

Shirley rubbed her shoulder. "You have to keep an eye out around here. There's always something interesting going on. Anyway, we were just going to close things down and start cleaning up."

"Sounds good," she said, yawning. "Buck wants me to be part of the grounds clean-up crew, too."

Shirley made a face. "Really? That's the *worst*!"

Mia didn't complain, though. As long as no one knew she was the one who'd been involved in the mugging, she'd happily clean the entire field, all night, if she had to. Because tomorrow, she was *really* going to have to keep an eye out.

CHAPTER TWENTY THREE

The following morning, Mia felt like the dead.

Bertie sounded the alarm to wake them at six a.m., which was late, compared to the day prior when they'd had to caravan down to Many. Still, Mia couldn't open her eyes. She was so exhausted from the night before, when she'd traveled every inch of the fairgrounds, picking up every last stray peanut, with only a small skeleton crew of helpers. She'd fallen into bed sometime after two in the morning, so tired she hadn't even bothered to brush her teeth.

"Hey," a faraway voice said, jostling her elbow. "Ro?"

She blinked and saw two of Shirley, sitting over her. Blinking more, she realized Shirley was fully dressed and made-up with her bright red lipstick. The rest of the women, too, were all ready to go.

Mia groaned. "Oh, God, is it morning already?"

Shirley nodded.

She tried to roll over. She just needed five more minutes of sleep, and then she'd be fine. She was sure of it. "Just—I'll skip breakfast," she mumbled.

Shirley's voice was tight, strained. "I would let you, Ro. But Buck's looking for you. He wants to see you before breakfast."

Mia sat straight up in bed, her first thought: *Oh, God, he's going to get on my case for a missed peanut.*

But her second thought was an even more worrisome one: *Someone told him what I did with that mugging. That's it. My cover's blown.*

She quickly got up, went to the wash area, and got cleaned up, then changed into a new t-shirt and jeans. When she reached the mess hall, she could hear the sounds of people chatting and eating their breakfasts. Johnny was just ducking his head out as she arrived. Again, he was dressed in head-to-toe black, and she had to admit, he had a very Johnny Cash vibe to him. Or was he more like Johnny Castle? Either way, Johnny Rose's name fit him.

"Hey, you," he said, looking just as worried as Shirley had sounded. "Buck has been asking for you. Come with me."

Her gut twisted as she followed him around the mess hall tent, to a small black trailer. Johnny went to the door and knocked, then twisted the latch and peeked in. "Found her," he said.

"It's about time. Bring her in here, now," Buck said. He didn't sound like he was in a very good mood.

She climbed the steps and went inside to find a small office with a single desk. Buck was sitting in an executive leather chair, piles of paper all around him, and smoking a cigar. He stubbed it out in an ashtray as she moved closer and fixed her with a narrow-eyed stare.

He didn't speak, so Mia felt the need to do so first: "Was there a problem with the cleaning I did after hours, sir?"

He glanced over at Johnny and laughed. Mia couldn't tell whether he was bitter or amused. "Don't play coy, missy. That's not what this is about. I think you know why I brought you in here, don't you?"

She shrugged innocently. "No, sir, I don't."

He shook his head. "I bet you don't. Now, girl, I told you before we don't care much where you've been or what you've done in the past, and I don't plan on looking into it. But I'd be lying if I said I wasn't just the slightest bit curious about your history."

She crossed her arms, as if that would disguise the fact that her heart was beating out of her chest. "I can't imagine why. I don't have anything in my past."

A slow smile spread over his face. "Right. And yet, according to reports, several people saw a little thing matching your description, disarming a thief last night. True?"

She started to shake her head, but he held up a hand.

"Don't give me that bullshit! We know it was you. The two victims described you to a tee."

"Maybe they were seeing things."

He leaned back in his chair. "What, are you thinking you're in trouble?" He pushed away and stood up, coming around the front of the desk. "No, you're a hero! If I had a medal, I'd pin it on you."

She hesitated, still not sure he was telling the truth. "You . . . would?"

"Sure! Steve—that's the carny you caught red-handed—was giving us problems since Amarillo. We had reports from carnival attendees and other carnies alike of things being stolen, but we just didn't know who was doing it. We had an idea it was him, but we needed evidence. And you, my dear, have provided that for us. So we owe you one."

She smiled uneasily. That was great, but she'd wanted to blend in. That wasn't exactly blending in. But if they owed her one, maybe that meant she could take it easier today? It wasn't that she was exhausted, though she was. If she was going to find this killer, she couldn't have her nose stuck to the grindstone, morning and night. She needed time to check things out.

"Thank you, sir," she said.

He put an arm around her back and led her to the door. "You go on. Have a second helping of oatmeal. On me." He smiled benevolently as Johnny opened the door for her.

"Thanks," she said, heading outside. So that was his way of rewarding her? More oatmeal? She didn't even like oatmeal. But it was probably better than them making a fuss. It would be better, actually, if they forgot her heroics, as soon as possible.

When she was outside, Johnny said, "Remind me not to get myself anywhere near that deadly right hook of yours. What are you, some kind of military?"

She shook her head. "I thought people didn't ask questions about other people."

"Right," he said as they walked to the mess hall. "But everyone's talking. You are the subject of quite a few rumors, whether you want to be or not."

Her stomach tightened. She definitely did not want to be. Luckily, the mess hall was cleared out by the time she went inside. She and Johnny got their oatmeal—and she got an extra scoop—and sat down at one of the long tables.

"So," Johnny said, digging into his food. "If you ain't talking about yourself, I guess I'll talk about myself."

He did, telling her about his youth in Brooklyn, and how he moved down to Texas when he was a teenager. He'd told all his friends in high school that he was going to run away to join the circus. They'd thought he was joking, but then he actually did. And he'd been working with Buck, first as a ride operator, and then as the assistant manager, for fifteen years.

"I like it," he said with a smile. "Most people can't deal with the long hours. The moving from place to place, and never setting down roots. But it never bothered me. I never wanted a family or any of that. We're a revolving door of help around here, so I'm probably the one who's been here longest."

“You’ve heard all the wild stories, then,” she said, wondering if he’d tell her the same thing Shirley had, about Bertie and Bo, in the restroom.

“I’ve heard good, bad, and ugly, for sure.”

“Really? So what’s the ugliest?”

He chuckled. “You only have to look around to see all the freaks we’ve got working here. Am I right?”

She had to agree with that. Most of the people she’d met didn’t look like your average, everyday citizen. They were the people on the fringe, the type of people who you wouldn’t want to be caught in a dark alley with. “Okay, so you’ve probably seen some pretty crazy things?”

He raised an eyebrow. “Sure have. But I guess it depends on your definition of crazy. I have enough stories to fill volumes, for sure.”

“Have you seen anything criminal?”

He snorted. “Of course.”

“Murders?”

Johnny finished scooping the last of his oatmeal out and stuffed it into his mouth. Mia had been so interested in the conversation, she hadn’t even started on her double helping. She wasn’t even hungry. As he swallowed, he said, “Oh, yeah. More than once.”

“Have you heard about murders of young couples? Possible serial killings?”

His eyes flashed to hers. He stiffened, and something about him seemed to shut down, as if the *welcome* sign in his eyes had suddenly been pulled in, the blinds shut tight. “Why? What have you heard?”

She shrugged nonchalantly and picked at a thread hanging from her shirt. “Oh, nothing much. I thought I heard someone mention a couple of young people who were killed, at a carnival stop, a few before this one.”

He frowned. “I don’t know anything about that,” he said shortly, grabbing his tray and standing abruptly, then heading for the door. He didn’t look back.

That meant only one thing to Mia. Johnny *did* know something, but it wasn’t something he was willing to tell. She’d need to find it out, some other way.

CHAPTER TWENTY FOUR

David Hunter rolled over, his head pounding, his neck stiff, and heard something crash beneath him.

He sat up and found himself lying on the couch in his living room, a few empty beer bottles scattered around him. The television was on, tuned to some golf show on ESPN. Rubbing his eyes, bits and pieces of last night came to him. He'd sent Louie off on his boy scout camping trip, then proceeded to come home, pop open a beer, and let everything fade into oblivion.

He sat up, massaging the kink out of his neck, and looked around. It was after ten in the morning. He'd had all these lofty ideas of really buckling down on his exercise routine during his leave of absence from the FBI. Lifting for hours every day, going on ten-mile runs, just like he had as a teen, getting back into tip-top bodybuilding shape.

But that had all fallen by the wayside as the days went on. It was guilt. Part of it was over being suspected by the higher-ups on the force. Part of it was that he felt like he wasn't doing enough to help Mia.

His eyes went to his laptop, lying on the ground, open and upside-down.

"Shit," he mumbled, leaning over to grab it. It must've fallen over while he slept. He tapped the keys, making sure it was still working.

It was, thank God. As he tapped, the screen came to life, illuminating the picture of one Lila Watkins.

Lila Watkins, the subject of a possible crime at a hotel that police officer Kevin Reynolds had been called to, who'd disappeared, a week later. She was a pretty girl, with long, dark hair and eyes, who probably could've been a model if she'd gone the right way.

In his research, he'd learned she'd just turned eighteen years old, the day before she disappeared. Her mother was a drug addict who was in jail, and so Lila was passed around through the foster care system for most of her young life. The little David had found out about her were a few mentions on adoption agency websites, looking to place Lila with a new family. Apparently, that had never happened, and she'd bounced from home to home.

Blinking to relieve himself of his double vision, he stood up and set the laptop on the coffee table. Then he got a bottle of water, sucking it down to get rid of the cottonmouth, and popped a few Excedrin in the bathroom.

Enough of this. I need to get back on the ball. So, gym first. Then a run, he thought, staring at his bloodshot eyes in the mirror as he closed the medicine cabinet.

But he couldn't bring himself to change into his workout outfit. He wasn't one of those people who loved working out, but usually he was able to prod himself into doing so by reminding himself of those post-workout endorphins that would power him through the rest of the day. That didn't work. He couldn't find the motivation.

Instead, he went back downstairs. When he returned to the living room he saw his open laptop. The screen should've gone to sleep by now, but for some reason, it hadn't, and Lila Watkins's eyes seemed to follow him across the room, saying, *Only you are looking for me. Find me.*

As if he needed anything else to feel guilty about.

Sighing, he sat down across from the laptop, cracked his knuckles, and got to work. He'd already Googled Lila Watkins's name and found very little. He knew that the FBI databases were likely off-limits, since they were watching his every move. But there were other things he could do as well, things he'd learned during his time as an agent.

He downloaded the photograph and plugged it in to an image search database. He knew it was a long-shot, as it wasn't an exact science—often, the photos that it retrieved were mere lookalikes to the source photograph. But it was worth a try.

When he clicked SEARCH PHOTO, a number of results came up. Many were clearly not Lila—they might've shared the same coloring or eye-shape as Lila, but it clearly wasn't her. But the first result was a 98% match.

And it was part of a website called Platinum Premier Girls, *your premier source for beautiful escorts in the Dallas-Fort Worth area.*

He navigated it to it, a sick feeling churning in his stomach. There, he saw many avatars of women in various suggestive positions, some in lingerie, some fully nude, each one giving the camera a come-hither gaze. The profile that matched the photograph he'd uploaded belonged to a girl named Kitty Lust. She was wearing a red bustier and short shorts, and posing suggestively on the hood of a red sportscar, but all the similarities were there.

It was, without a doubt, Lila Watkins.

He read the profile of the girl, feeling guilty just for staring at the photographs, each one more suggestive than the other. Though the service said that its girls were all adults, Lila had been a member for a few years, seeing clients, which meant that she'd somehow been able to fake her age.

Maybe one of her clients had been Senate hopeful Wilson Andrews.

It was a definite possibility. Despite his squeaky-clean image, there were underground rumors of his womanizing ways. Some said that his sexual appetite was impossible to satisfy.

If Wilson Andrews had seen her while underage, and she'd attempted to tell someone . . . he'd have a good motive for her disappearance.

But how could David prove that?

He scrolled down. Turned out, Kitty Lust had a number of solid reviews, most with acronyms he didn't really understand. The few he did seemed to really love Kitty:

AAA+++! Beautiful, Busty and Sweet!

She's going to be my go-to girl whenever I'm in the Dallas area.

I love her curves. She's sweet and accommodating. Wish I could've stayed with her longer.

There were dozens. She didn't have a single bad review. Of course, the users had names like *JoinTexas, Hot2Trot, and BillyBobT* with avatars of parts of their anatomy or cartoon characters. It was probably too much to hope for a photograph of Wilson Andrews, with *WAndrews—Texas's next state senator!* underneath.

His eyes caught on another photograph of her. In it, the girl was sitting on the edge of a bed in a bikini, her body on display, but there was a sad vulnerability in her eyes. A look that said, *I don't really want to be doing this.* He rubbed the side of his face. Poor girl. She was thrown into this world, way too young, and objectified, like a piece of meat. She was never really loved a day in her life.

Someone like her could easily be disposed of, and no one would've noticed or cared.

And that interested him very much.

The escort website, he noticed, also had a networking feature, where clients could refer other clients so that the girls remained safe during their gigs. It looked like the last time that Kitty Lust had logged on was over a year ago. She'd left a couple of public messages on the profiles of a few other girls. On a photo posted by a girl named

Summer Rain, she'd posted, "*On fire!*" and to another provider who'd been asking whether a certain potential client was kosher, she'd written, "*Not bad. Clean. Talks a little too much but good tipper.*"

David clicked on the profile of Summer Rain. She was an exotic girl with pouty lips and waist-length, light-brown hair, which she used in her photographs to strategically cover parts of her anatomy. A little blinking light said, *Online now! Chat with Summer!* He opened a message to her and a dialogue box popped up: *You must be logged in to send Summer Rain a Message.*

Quickly, he created a profile, calling himself AgentDH, and choosing a black screen as an avatar. When he finished, she was still online, so he typed in:

AgentDH: Hi, SummerRain, can I ask you a question?

She replied right away.

SummerRain: $200 for the hour. I'm booked up the weekend but I have an opening mid-week.

He almost laughed. *And it's really nice to meet you, too.*

AgentDH: I'm not interested in booking you. I just have a question about another girl you might have known.

A long pause. Then:

SummerRain: Are you a cop?

Shit. He realized, too late, that he probably shouldn't have used any handle that in any way related to his being part of law enforcement.

AgentDH: No. Just a friend of someone, and I want to see her come home.

He waited, so long he thought she must've gotten spooked and decided to block him. Just as he was about to change his nickname and try the other girl, a message came up:

SummerRain: You mean Lila.

He stared at the message. She hadn't said, *You mean Kitty.* Which meant that she probably knew her in real life. That was very interesting.

AgentDH: That's right. Do you know her?

SummerRain: Yeah, we went to school together. She got me into this. We've done a few gigs together.

AgentDH: When was the last time you saw her?

He waited, wondering if she was going to respond. Then she said:

SummerRain: A week before she disappeared. She was going to meet a new client at the hotel. I never heard from her after that. I know people tried to contact her. I called her, but she never answered. It's like she dropped off the face of the earth.

AgentDH: Did she say anything about that new client?

SummerRain: Only that he was big-time and she thought he had to be loaded. He'd offered her two-thousand for the night.

Big-time. Wealthy. That had Wilson Andrews written all over it.

AgentDH: And you never heard from her after that?

SummerRain: No, I even messaged her to ask how it went and she didn't respond.

Possibly because after that encounter, she was running scared. Maybe she was being threatened. Maybe she'd attempted to step away from everything, because she knew she was in danger. He was about to thank her when another message came through.

SummerRain: I almost considered packing it in when the same thing happened to Whitney, six months later.

AgentDH: Who is Whitney?

SummerRain: Whoops, I'm sorry—BlondeBunny99. She was another friend of mine. And she went through the same thing. Told me she had a well-paying client one night; the next night, gone.

He navigated to the search bar and looked up BlondeBunny, only to see a girl with pigtails and a pink teddy, smiling seductively at the screen. God, how many of these poor girls were there? She couldn't have been older than twenty, either. He checked her profile to see the last time she'd logged in, but it had been dormant since six months ago. A bunch of commenters on her profile had posted things like, *Where you at?* and *Hope you're doing well, wherever you are, sweetheart!* Someone had posted, *The rumor is, she got out of the business.* ☹

But had she? Or had she suffered the same fate as Lila? Disappeared, both online and in the real world?

AgentDH: You have Whitney's last name?

SummerRain: Nope—not doing this. You're freaking me out dude. I'm reporting your profile.

He thought about responding, but it didn't matter. He had all the information he needed.

Downloading Whitney's photograph, he uploaded it to his image search database. There wasn't any exact match, but one match hit upon something that piqued his interest.

It was an article in the *Dallas Morning News,* from five months ago. *Friends Looking for Answers in Disappearance of Dallas Teen.*

Sure enough, there was a smiling photograph of the same blonde girl that had been wearing a teddy on the escort webpage. In this picture, though, she was wearing a cap and gown. Her name was

Whitney Rollins, and she'd been missing for six months. According to the article, she'd left that evening to go on a date, and never returned. Her roommates had reported her missing, a couple days later.

Had that last fateful "date" been an arranged meeting with Wilson Andrews?

Possibly. This woman, too, seemed to have no relations. Though she had a couple of roommates, she didn't have any family in the area. Besides that one article, there was nothing else mentioning the poor girl. Concern about Whitney Rollins's whereabouts had simply evaporated as time went on, and the case had gone cold.

David couldn't deny the similarities between these two cases. Lila and Whitney. Two young, beautiful escorts, who advertised their services on the same website, and simply vanished. Not to mention that neither seemed to have anyone who'd miss them when they were gone. It seemed to be more than a coincidence. Were there others?

If he was in the office, he'd simply pull a database of all the missing young girls in the Dallas area from the past year. But he couldn't do that right now without arousing suspicion with Pembroke. So he Googled it himself, coming up with a fairly good list. He'd find the girls' photographs and see if any of them had listed services on the website.

It was a rabbit hole. But one he was happy to go down, if it would help him find out dirt on Wilson Andrews.

CHAPTER TWENTY FIVE

That afternoon, as Mia walked up and down the aisles of the carnival, offering help wherever she could, she got the definite feeling that news of her act of heroism had spread. By lunchtime, she had the feeling all eyes were on her, which wasn't a good thing.

Mia sighed as she helped a couple of carnies move the fortune-telling tent to a different spot. Supposedly, the fortune-teller, who on some nights was Bertie but on other nights was whoever wanted to fill in, hadn't made a lot of money the night prior, and Buck had been upset because he thought it had to do with location. So his orders were to move it to a more visible spot, next to the carousel. He was in a frenzy, ordering all the carnies around, so they were all flapping about like chickens with their heads cut off.

As she pulled a tent stake out, someone behind her called, "There goes Supergirl." At first, she thought they couldn't have been talking about her, until another carny said, "Be careful, you don't want to mess with her," to his pal and pointed directly at her as they made their way through the fairway.

She groaned and turned to find Bertie, heading purposely for her. "You're moving the tent, Rolanda?"

Mia nodded. "Buck said he wanted me to—"

"Here," she said, shoving a pile of black fabric and lace into Mia's arms. Mia realized as she held it in her hands that it was a long dress, with many layers and a crinoline.

"What is this?"

"It's Madame Zola's costume. You're It."

She shook her head. "Oh, I couldn't—"

"Sure you can. I ran it past Buck and he's all for it. Said I did a crappy job last night and no one wanted to pay. So—"

"Oh, but that was because the tent was in a poor location," she pointed out.

Bertie shook her head. "Doesn't matter. He's fed up with me. Thinks his new Supergirl could do better."

She stared at the dress. It occurred to her to apologize for taking Bertie's role, but Bertie seemed more relieved than anything to be rid of it. "Okay. Well, I have to get the tent up first, and—"

"I've got to get back to Buck. He's having an issue with the ticket printer," she said, already several yards away, not turning around.

Mia looked over the dress and groaned. Great. She'd thought the food truck was a bad vantage point from which to catch a killer. In a tent, closed off from the rest of the carnival? She wouldn't see anything.

She dragged the stake to the new location and dug it into the soft earth. As she worked it deeper into the ground, she looked around. When she'd escaped, months ago, her number one rule to avoid detection was simple—never stay long in the same place. She'd already been with the carnival a couple of days. She couldn't stay much longer and hope to avoid trouble.

Time was running out. Tonight could be her only chance.

She'd have to find a way to step out of the tent, now and then, to look around.

The only problem was, where? She was still no closer to having a definite suspect. And people in the carnival weren't willing to talk. Not only was Johnny reluctant to mention anything about the murdered couples from the other towns, but it seemed like everyone was either playing dumb or downright hostile about it, shutting her down even before the question came out of her mouth. But there was something behind it. She was sure about it. She was sure those murders had a tie to the carnival.

Mia wiggled the pole, trying to dig it deeper into the ground, but even after a few minutes, it still hadn't gotten very far. She looked around for the other carnies who'd agreed to help her, but they'd all gone off to help Buck with other tasks. As she was about to give up, she heard the creaking sound of the cotton candy cart, being wheeled into place.

When it came into view, she saw a familiar face. Will.

"Hey, Will," she called to the teenager, who was wearing all-black, his face still mostly covered by the loose hood of his sweatshirt. He didn't look up, so she called louder. "Will, can you give me a hand?"

He continued to wheel the cart down the aisle, ignoring her.

She rolled her eyes. So, he was going to play it this way. Fine. She walked over to him and stood in front of his path. "Hello, Will?"

He continued to wheel the cart slowly, until she thought he might ram it into her. When he was almost about to, he stopped and said, "Why do you need help? Aren't you the super-hero? That's what Buck's calling you."

She crossed her arms. "I do need help getting the tent up. Please? The carnival's going to start in a few minutes and everyone who was helping me ditched me."

He sighed and let go of the cart. "Fine. What do you need?"

She led him to the tent. "Can you help me get these stakes in so that I can start setting up the tent?"

He didn't answer, but he set to work, moving the poles into the dirt.

Since he was her captive audience, she thought she might as well ask him questions. Not that Will, ray of sunshine that he was, would answer. "So, are you working the cotton candy cart tonight?"

He grunted what she thought was a "yes."

"I did the food truck last night," she said, hoping that she could actually have a civil conversation with him as she began to set up the poles for the rest of the tent. "It was kind of hot and exhausting. Now, I have to be the fortune teller."

He looked over at the dress she'd set on the circular fortune-telling table and smirked. "That job sucks."

"Does it?"

He nodded. "No one wants to do it. You get some real weirdos who think what you're telling is like, real. And if you don't tell them what they want to hear, they'll go batshit on you. One of 'em even attacked Bertie." He finished digging the pole in and tested it. "You'll be fine though. You're Supergirl."

"I'm not," she said, gnawing on her lip. "And now you're making me nervous. Can I trade with you?"

She could've sworn she saw him smile. It was over in a flash, though. "You want me to be Madame Zola?"

"Yeah. You could do it, probably."

"Hell, no."

"Well, what's your dad doing?" Mia asked, looking around for Frank. "You think he'd trade with me?"

Will hooked a thumb over his shoulder. "He's at the dunk tank."

She winced. "Oh, no thanks."

"He isn't *in* the dunk tank. That's Johnny. My dad just runs the stand and gives people the balls and stuff."

Mia tapped her chin. That didn't sound so bad. "Think he'd—"

"Hell, no. You're stuck there." And this time, he really did grin. For a moment, she wondered why she'd even suspected him in the first place. The boy was clearly just a regular teenager—a little awkward and antisocial, but by no means evil.

She laughed as she finished tying down the end of the tent. "All right, all right." She saw her opening, and she took it. "Everything's okay with your dad, right?"

"What do you mean?" He gave her a blank look.

"Well, I saw him yelling at you. It made me wonder if—"

"Yeah. It's good. That's just my dad. He has one volume. Loud. Probably from the army."

"Oh. Okay. Just wanted to check to make sure you were okay." She stepped back and looked at her handiwork. It looked good. Dusting her hands off on the back of her jeans, she grabbed the dress. "Thanks for your help. Do you think you can roll the table in for me? I have to get changed into this terrible getup, I guess."

He nodded, and she went over to the women's tent to change, looking everywhere for something suspicious. Something that would lead her to the killer.

Unfortunately, there was nothing to see. Just dozens of carnies, running around, getting ready for showtime.

*

The dress was *beyond* ridiculous.

Bertie's frame was clearly a lot smaller than Mia's, because she felt like she was bursting out of it. She had to leave a couple of buttons open at the chest in order to make it fit, and so she looked like a cheap Wild West harlot. Not only that, but it didn't do enough to cover her sneakered feet. So much for not attracting attention. As she walked back to the tent, she felt like everyone was staring at her, and with good reason.

Inside the darkened tent, Will was just finishing setting everything up. He'd arranged the string lights as expertly as they'd been placed in the previous location, and had even set up the crystal ball and fringed curtains that gave the tent an authentic look.

"Nice job," she remarked. She would've given him a pat on the back if she wasn't sure he'd probably flinch away. "Couldn't have done it better myself. Thanks."

He grunted and headed for the tent opening, but hesitated there.

Then he turned around suddenly. He was gnawing on his lip, as if he had something to say, but was unsure whether to say it.

Mia sat down on the folding chair behind the table. "Is everything all right?"

For a second, she thought he might ask to have his fortune told. But then he said, "You were asking about them, weren't you? About those two people who were killed in Canton?"

She stared at him. So people had been talking. Wondering why she was asking, likely, and probably putting an even bigger target on her back. "Yes, I was."

"Why?"

"No reason in particular. I was interested in the carnival's history. And I heard someone mention it."

He fidgeted from one foot to the other. Did he know something about the murders? Before she could ask, he said, "I saw them. Right before they were killed."

She blinked. "You did? Are you sure?"

"Of course I'm sure," he snapped, apparently upset that she would doubt him. "Couldn't believe it when I saw their pictures in the news, the next day. But it was them."

"Where did you see them?"

"I work the cotton candy cart a lot of times, so I see a lot of things. And I saw them, walking together by the Ferris wheel. They got on it and were making out, practically swallowing each other's heads. I remember it because I'd thought it was pretty nasty, how they were practically going at it, in public."

Mia's eyes narrowed at that description. Hadn't Momma said that Katty Powell, the female victim's mother, believed they weren't serious? That sounded pretty serious. But then again, mothers didn't always know what their daughters were up to. Maybe they had been very in love.

And if they were, a suicide pact was again a possibility.

"Another reason I remember it was because it was the last ride of the night, and they got stuck at the top of the Ferris wheel. Right up there at the very top. And I remember thinking to myself, *Who knows what the hell they're doing up there, where no one can see them?* It was late, I just wanted to close things down and get to bed. But I remembered thinking that if they had to fix the Ferris wheel, I might never be able to turn in." He backed toward the entrance to the tent and lifted the flap.

"Wait, Will. Did you see what happened to them when they got off? Was anyone following them?"

He shook his head. "Not that I saw. They were joking a little that it'd been fun, trying to make the cart rock back and forth. Still swallowing each other's heads. Then they disappeared into the crowd that was heading for the exit. We were all trying to round everyone up, to get them to leave, so there was a lot of chaos. The next time I heard anything about them, they'd been found dead." He let out a deep breath. "The lake was on the other side of the parking lot. Must've walked there to get some more, you know, *private time.* Guess someone followed them, or he killed her and then himself, or whatever. Who knows?"

She rested her elbows on the tablecloth, digesting this information. Will might've been one of the last people to see Mari and Tobias alive in Canton. And now she knew where they'd been, right before they'd headed for the exit.

But what did it mean?

Will poked his head out. "I gotta go. They're letting people in."

He slipped out without saying goodbye. It was showtime. It would've probably been a good idea to think of some standard predictions she could give to her customers, but instead, her mind stayed firmly on the Ferris wheel. It wasn't far away, just the next row over. She might even be able to walk out the back of the tent and look at it.

As she sat there, fingers laced in front of her, she realized she should've asked Will who the Ferris wheel operator was. Maybe whoever it was saw something, too.

Or maybe . . .

A strange sense prickled the back of her neck. Another thing she should've asked Will—had he seen anything in Lookout Point?

I need to talk to him. Now, she thought, rising from her chair.

Just as she did, a young couple stepped into the tent. The girl, who couldn't have been more than sixteen, was giggling and holding a bag of cotton candy. "Hi, are you Madame Zola?' she asked, giving Mia a once-over with typical teenage attitude that said she wasn't impressed.

"Yeah," Mia barked, disappointed, then sighed and sat back down. "I mean, yes, children, come in. I will reveal all."

The acne-faced teen in the football jersey squeezed the girl's side. "Go on, Luc. Learn your future."

She sat down and laid a crumpled ten dollar bill on the table. Mia wasn't even sure what the price was—it was written on a sign outside, but she hadn't really been paying attention. "I don't really believe in any of this hocus pocus," she said, snapping her gum.

"It is my job to make you believe," Mia said, reaching for her hand. She studied the girl's hand and said, "You will take a great trip."

She nodded and blew a bubble with her pink bubble gum, letting it pop on her face. "I'm going to University of Alabama next fall. Roll Tide!"

Mia nodded, "I see great opportunity in your future, but you must keep your eyes open to it."

As Mia held the girl's hand, the couple began to theorize what that could mean. Meanwhile, Mia had begun to think about her own opportunity, slipping through her fingers. She felt close to the answer to this case, very close. But she had to talk to Will.

The teenagers stared at her, expectant, waiting for the rest of her future to be read. Her mind blank of wise fortune-cookie prognostications to appease them, she spit out, "And you'll make so many people proud with the noble profession you pursue."

The girl wrinkled her nose. "Noble? I was going to major in graphic design."

Mia looked more closely at her hand, as if it held the answers. "Well . . . I can't be sure. Maybe you change majors?"

The girl blinked. "Should I?" She looked over at her boyfriend. "You think this means I should?"

Great, now not only was she letting a killer get away, but she might be responsible for ruining a girl's future. "I don't know, I wouldn't take too much stock in it," she said weakly, as Will's words repeated in her head: *They were joking a little that it'd been fun, trying to make the cart rock back and forth. Still swallowing each other's heads.*

Suddenly, it hit her.

She let go of the girl's hand, reached into the pocket of the dress and pulled out her cell phone. It only had a little bit of charge left. She navigated to Facebook, completely forgetting the teens across the table from her until the girl cleared her throat.

"Uh, is that all?"

Mia looked up. "Yes . . . that and, you will have a long and happy life," she added, looking back at her phone.

The girl stood up, face red. "You're like, the worst fortune teller I've ever been to."

“Ruby!” the guy said, behind her. “Don’t be rude.”

“What? She is,” Ruby said indignantly. “I don’t even think she’s a real psychic.”

Mia almost laughed. *Gee, what gave it away*? She handed her money back to her. “Yeah, sorry. If you’re looking for a real psychic, you probably shouldn’t come to a carnival. I apologize that you weren’t satisfied,” she said with a placating smile. Buck would be upset, but whatever.

The girl took her money back, stuffed it in the pocket of her shorts, and left with a short, “Huh.”

Mia hoped she’d tell her friends, so that she’d have an easy night. Unfortunately, when she got to the front of the tent to look for Will, she saw a long queue, stretching halfway across the fairway. If Buck was looking for a good location to put the fortune-telling tent, he’d clearly found it.

She looked at the first woman in line, a middle-aged woman wearing a *DON’T MESS WITH TEXAS!* t-shirt. Another soon-to-be-dissatisfied customer, likely, and if her t-shirt was any indication, this could get ugly. She held up a finger. “Would you mind waiting here, for one moment?”

The woman frowned. “How much longer?”

“Just a minute.” Mia went back into the tent and grabbed her phone, navigating to what she’d been hoping to get a look at, before. Jason Delaney-Sawyer’s Instagram page. It was the final selfie of him and his girlfriend Kiki, with their faces smushed together, smiling for the camera, with the treetops and the dark sky behind them. She scanned to the caption: *#rockinandrollin,* realization dawning.

Oh, my God. They’re on the Ferris Wheel. Just like the kids from Canton had been, right before they’d been killed.

She spun in the chair to look at the back of the tent, in the direction of the Ferris wheel. Was there some connection between their deaths and the ride? Was the operator of the ride watching them? Had he made the ride stop up there, at the very top, so he could observe them? And then, when they came down, had he killed them?

Out near the front of the tent, a voice called, “Hello? Madame Zola? You alive in there?” It sounded like *DON’T MESS WITH TEXAS.* If she didn’t start letting customers in, either they’d kill her, or Buck would.

But she couldn't wait. From the sound of the calliope, the shouts and voices rising up outside, the carnival was in full-swing. She didn't have much time.

Making the decision, she lifted the curtains and felt around the back of the tent for the back opening. When she found it, she slipped out into the back aisle, where the tent abutted the back of another, the face-painting tent. As she crept along it to its front, a couple of kids, sitting on stools, having their faces made up to look like tigers and princesses, looked up at her. "Who's that, Mommy?" one of the girls asked in fright. "Maleficent?"

"No, honey, no, it's all right!" her mother soothed, giving Mia the evil-eye for scaring her child.

Mia stepped past it as quickly as she could. Just beyond it, she saw the brightly-lit wheel, spinning. Night had already fallen, though, and now, she couldn't see who was standing at its base, operating the controls.

She rushed for it, bobbing and weaving through the crowds, the families with balloon-wielding kids and enormous double-strollers, the throngs of teenagers huddling together in tight packs, the older folks with their giant scooters. It was only when she reached the base of the wheel that she noticed who was standing at the control panel.

Mia skidded to a stop at the steps to the platform, and her jaw dropped open.

CHAPTER TWENTY SIX

Back again in Canton, Kane Wilcox sat at a table at Momma's restaurant, finally eating the home-cooked dinner he'd put off far too long—chicken and dumplings— and thinking over the details of the two cases he was sure Mia North was pursuing. He hated having to retrace his steps, but he was sure he was missing something. And so his only answer was to look back at the two cases and see what he might have overlooked.

But he'd been in Canton all day, talking with people close to the case, the local PD, friends, and family, and he'd gotten nowhere. The police didn't even think it was a crime—they seemed to think it was a suicide pact. Some friends agreed with it, some didn't.

As he sat there, reviewing his notes, Momma came by and slid a plate with a giant slice of blueberry pie on the table. "Honey, you looked like you could use this," she said with a smile, picking up his empty dinner plate. "Can I get you some coffee?"

He nodded. "Thanks." It was going to be another long night. Forget about getting home, nice and fast, to Dana. If things kept on like this, he'd be lucky to see her again this month. Before Momma could turn to leave, he said, "Hey. Ma'am. You spoke to that woman, the other day, about those murders? The ones at Two Acre Lake?"

She nodded. "Right. The woman who was as sweet as pie? Still hot on her tail? Or cold? I wager you didn't find her yet?"

"No, I did not. Can you remember, exactly, what you told her?"

Momma shrugged. "She mentioned something about those deaths not being suicides—that was the rumor. And I told her I agreed with that. I told her that I know Mari's mom, Katty Powell, and that Katty was beside herself when her daughter died."

He wrote that down in the margin of his notebook. *Katty Powell.* He'd attempted to talk to the victim's mother during his investigations, but she never answered her door or returned any of the voicemails he'd left. Either she was in mourning, or she was avoiding him. "Anything else?"

"Yeah. I told her Mari was accepted to college, Tulane, and that there was no sign she was depressed. The police said it was a suicide pact, but Katty said that was ridiculous because she'd only been dating the boy a couple weeks. It wasn't serious."

"Anything else?"

"Well, she asked about the boy Mari was seeing. Tobias. She asked if it was possible he killed Mari, and turned the gun on himself. But I said Katty didn't think it was. The boy passed Katty's strict requirements."

He nodded. He'd spoken with Tobias's mother, who'd thought it couldn't be a suicide, either. No one he'd spoken with actually believed that either of the two kids were responsible, so in this way, it was similar to the case at Lookout Point. "This Katty . . . can I talk with her?"

Momma shook her head. "Well, you could. But I haven't seen her around. She's mourning over poor Mari. Personally, I think she got tired of everyone talking about it and decided to leave town for a while."

He nodded. Dragging his hands down his face, he watched out the window as the sun continued to set. Another day, chasing all over town, for absolutely nothing. "So let me ask you a question," he said, digging his fork into the pie. "What do you think happened? You think it was a random murderer?"

Momma sighed. "I can't say for sure. Canton is so safe, usually. But yes, it seems like it. People come from far and wide to go to our flea markets, and so we get a number of outsiders. Drifters, who commit crimes." She shrugged.

He dropped his fork, stiffening. Mia was on the case for some reason. What was he missing?

"Maybe it had something to do with the carnival?" she said. "A lot of drifters come in for that."

He looked up. "Carnival?"

She pointed to a sign. *FunTime Amusements Carnival.*

He thought about it. A traveling carnival. That actually made sense. "Do you know where that carnival went to?"

"Actually, now that you mention it, I do. One of the carnies came in here. He said they were off to Louisiana. A place called Many."

"Many?" This was looking better and better. He pushed away from the table, jumped to his feet, and went for his wallet, throwing a couple of twenties down on the table. "I've got to go."

“You haven’t eaten your pie yet!” Momma called after him.

But he’d already gone for the door. He needed to check into this new hunch. If it was right, he knew exactly why Mia had crossed the border to Louisiana. And now, again, he was hot on her tail.

CHAPTER TWENTY SEVEN

The man stood at the controls, looking up at the spinning wheel, now lit with blue and red lights. He thought for a moment about his long-time fantasy—holding hands with the woman of his dreams as they took the wheel up to the top. Waiting as the operator brought the wheel to a stop, to let more people on. Sneaking kisses in the dark, above the bright excitement of the carnival.

No, he'd never had that. All those times, he'd asked girls for the opportunity, and they'd declined. Some had even laughed at him. Some had been angry that he'd even thought he could be a possible match for them. They'd said, "You? I'd rather die," and other mean things that ripped at his heart. His father had abused him at home, getting out the strap whenever he did anything wrong—and the girls abused him at school.

It was like a tornado, swirling inside him, growing stronger and stronger. The rage. He thought it would consume him. And then—

Mary. Mary Violet.

That was her name. A beautiful name, for a beautiful person, with sparkling green eyes and the softest, most lovely brown hair he'd ever seen. She'd said yes, almost even before he asked.

But they'd never gotten to go to the carnival. He'd bought her flowers. Dressed to the nines. Made sure everything was perfect, for her.

And then, when he arrived on her doorstep to take her out, he learned the truth from her distraught mother. She'd drowned. The night before. In the lake, behind her house. A swimming accident, they'd said. So sudden. Mary was gone.

With her, all of his dreams of his perfect life were gone, too.

Now, as he watched the wheel slow to a stop, he sucked in a breath and wished the urge would go away. Before, he'd hoped to control it, but now it felt like it was about to blow its top off. His hand shook on the control as he pressed the button to slow down the ride.

He watched as a young couple, probably no more than eighteen, approached, tickets in hand. The boy was wearing a football jersey, the girl had long blonde braids. They handed the tickets off carelessly, the girl giggling something about how that fortune teller was a rip-off.

"I'll tell your fortune," he shouted at her, grabbing her hand as they sat on the bench.

The man knew what would happen next, what always happened. He'd observed and rehearsed it in his head, again and again, like a script from a favorite play. They'd go up to the very top of the wheel. The boy would undoubtedly try to swing the cart back and forth and, frightened, the girl would cling to him. And then, while she was in his arms, he'd duck his head and kiss her.

It worked every time. By the time they stepped off the ride, they'd both be red-faced, exhilarated, grinning from ear to ear with their dreamy, lovesick smiles.

He scowled at the thought as he watched the young couple, so in love, climbing to the top of the wheel. They didn't even know he existed. No, they were so in love, they didn't know the rest of the *world* existed.

How he hated them. How sickening they were. They didn't deserve any of that happiness. No. They didn't deserve to breathe air.

They needed to die.

CHAPTER TWENTY EIGHT

Mia hesitated at the stairs to the Ferris wheel, shocked. She began to take a step backwards, hoping the crowd would swallow her up, but that wasn't an easy feat in her show-stopping black dress.

She knew it was too late when the man at the controls of the Ferris Wheel turned and caught sight of her. "Rolanda?"

She froze. "Buck?"

Almost as if they'd rehearsed it for weeks, they both said, at the exact same time. "What are you doing here?"

It didn't compute. Was Buck, the big man in charge, the murderer of those teens? He'd seemed a little bossy, yes. Angry and irrational, too. But a murderer? No, he was more of a businessman, overly concerned with making FunTime a success. And probably the last thing a business needed was to have murders associated with it. Maybe he had a dissociative disorder. Maybe he didn't realize he was the killer, couldn't control himself. Or . . .

Or maybe her theory was wrong from the start.

Buck's ears turned bright red, and his face followed, indicating he was about to blow. He fiddled with the controls to stop the wheel, smiled stiffly to take a man and his toddler daughter's tickets and help them onto the next available cart, then turned to her, shaking his head.

"What the hell are you doing here, girl?" he growled under his breath, still smiling for his customers to see. "Why aren't you at the fortune-telling tent?"

"Why are *you* here?" she countered. "You don't run the Ferris Wheel."

He laughed bitterly and stopped the ride again. "You think I don't know that? The regular operator's playing sick. Something about a stomach bug. I think he just ate too many free corn dogs, the fat-ass."

"Who is the regular ride operator?"

"Randy," he snarled.

Randy. He was the large man who'd been in the van when they'd come here, the talkative one with the annoying laugh. Curiously, though, she hadn't seen him at all since the ride down.

Maybe he wasn't sick. Maybe that was just an excuse.

Maybe he was stalking and killing a couple, right now.

Looking around frantically, she barked out, "Where is he? Did you see where he went?"

"No," he said, finishing loading up a couple of kids into the next cart, and starting the wheel to turn again. "Why don't you quit worrying about everyone else and get your ass back to the fortune telling tent? You want to get yourself fired, girl? You might've stopped that mugging last night, but that don't mean you can do anything you want. I have a mind to dock your pay, at the very least."

She shook her head. "No . . ." she said, mostly to appease him. If she got fired, so be it. She needed to get out of Buck's sight and find Randy, as quickly as possible. "I'll go back there," she lied.

"Good," he called, as she picked up the skirts of her dress and broke into a run. She didn't get far because the crowds were thick, swarming all over the fairway. She dodged them, making like she was heading back to the fortune-telling tent, and then, when she was out of Buck's view, veered in the opposite direction, keeping an eye out for Randy.

The crowd broke apart, and she noticed a clown with a pink dress, walking on stilts. She ran to it, not sure who was under all that make-up. "Hey! Have you seen Randy?"

"Rolanda?" the voice from high above her head said, staring down at her.

She squinted, trying to make out the features under all that white goop. When she saw whiskers, it hit her. "Greg? Is that you?"

"Guilty as charged!" he said, waving at bunch of little boys who walked by. "But right now, I'm Long-Legged Lucy. I see you got roped into being Madame Zola. Who're you looking for?"

Surprised, she almost lost track of her purpose. "Uh, Randy? Have you seen him?"

He shrugged. "No. If he's missing, he's probably in the mess hall. That's where you'll usually find him."

"Thanks," she said hurriedly, brushing past him and into the crowd, diving into every open space as she tried to weave her way through the throng.

She ducked under the temporary fencing, where it was staff only, and finally clear of people she rushed toward the mess hall tent. When she got there, though, it was mostly empty, except for a few carnies she didn't know, and old Bo, who was sitting at a table, taking his break. "What's gotten you in such a rush, little lady?" he said to her.

"I'm looking for Randy. Have you seen him?" Her words came out in a rush as she scanned the food line, hoping to find him there.

He nodded. "I did, on my way over here. He wasn't feeling well. Was on his way to the toilets."

"The toilets?" She grimaced and turned on her heel, calling, "Thanks!"

Without thinking, she ran to the line of about ten porta-potties, set up at the far end of the fairway. People were waiting, but she ran in front of them, and started knocking on each door. "Randy?" she called.

"Hey!" a woman with her children shouted. "There's a line!"

"I know, I'm just looking for someone," she called over her shoulder, knocking on the next one, just as the door opened and a little boy came out, giving her a curious look.

By the time she got halfway down the line, she felt discouraged. If he was really stalking a young couple, he wouldn't be hanging out in the potty. That would've been just an excuse, his way to avoid work so that he could commit his crime without anyone being the wiser. And if he was committing that crime, where would he be?

She sighed and looked around. *Obviously not here, dummy. Stop running around like an idiot. Think for a second.*

Mia wandered away from the potties, head down, trying to put herself in the shoes of the killer. If he was targeting young people, watching them on the Ferris wheel, he must've seen a couple, watching them like a hawk as they took their ride. He'd watch them go around and around. He'd like that. That whole ride would be like an appetizer to him, getting him primed for the main event, when he'd follow them off into a secluded place and murder them.

She blinked as something came to her.

If he really did love watching these young couples ride the Ferris wheel, the controls of the Ferris wheel would be a terrible place to be. Near the base, he wouldn't be able to see the kids, going around, reaching the top of the wheel. No, it wouldn't be a good vantage point at all.

A better one would be at a booth or a ride across the way.

Mia turned to face the carnival. From where she stood, she could only see the tents, facing away from her. She stared at the ground, thinking hard, bringing the map of the carnival to her mind, trying to remember what attraction had been set up, directly across from the wheel. She'd seen it, in passing, as she was dragging the fortune telling tent to its new location, but what was it? And more importantly, who was manning it?

It came to her in a rush.

Of course. It was the dunk tank. The attraction Frank, Will's father, was supposedly working at.

Grabbing her skirts, she took off like a bullet, heading back into the crowds, hoping she wasn't too late.

CHAPTER TWENTY NINE

By now, the crowds only seemed to have increased, but Mia was able to make it through more easily. Part of it was that the fireworks display would be soon, and so people were finding places to sit so that they could watch the show.

As she made it past the tents, she noticed the line in front of the fortune-telling booth had broken up. That probably meant she didn't have a job anymore, but she didn't care. She'd already had it in her mind that this was the last night she could spend with this traveling carnival. If Agent Wilcox was worth his salt, he'd probably gotten hold of news of her near-arrest in Mansfield. That meant that he might be right on her tail.

She couldn't be worried about that, now, though. She had a murderer to find.

As she tore through the crowd, toward the dunking booth, she hoped that this time her hunch was right.

The booth came into view, with a long line of people, waiting to try their luck. As she reached it, a teenage boy in a backwards baseball cap threw a line-drive that hit the target, square in the center. The platform instantly gave way, and the poor guy on it fell into the tank of frothing water. People cheered in glee, and the kid high-fived his friends.

Mia stopped short, taking in Frank. The bald man was poised there, leaning against a post, his hand on his hip. He motioned to the next kid, taking his money and handing him three baseballs as they waited for the platform to be reset.

Mia watched him closely, waiting for him to look back at the Ferris wheel. Of course, as the killer, he'd glance that way, now and again. He'd be interested in the couples, riding it.

But he didn't. He kept his eyes squarely on the next customer as he explained the rules of the game.

Doubt flooded in. Had she been wrong?

"Hey," a voice said behind her, and she was aware of the creak of a snack cart. "You get lost on the way to your tent?"

She startled to find Will standing there. "Oh, Will, I—" She stopped. *I was just going to confront your father for murdering those teenagers.*

"You look like you saw a ghost," he said, as a little girl came up to him with a dollar, for cotton candy. He grabbed a bag of it and handed it to her. "Was being Madame Zola that bad?"

She shook her head, still watching Frank, waiting, hoping that he'd turn around and glance at the Ferris wheel and make her theory true. But he didn't. And now that she thought about it, she didn't *want* it to be true. The last thing she wanted was to see Frank apprehended for murder in front of his young son.

"No," she said, managing a smile. "It wasn't. How's your night going?"

He shrugged. "Not bad."

She was only half-listening, because she'd been knocked back a few pegs, closer to square one. The fireworks display at the end of the night was coming up, and it would be prime time for the killer to appear. But Frank, she decided, was probably not him.

Then who was it?

"Na na na na na!" a voice chortled. "You suck!"

Will laughed. "He's the worst."

Mia was stirred from her thoughts by the commotion and Will's laugh. She realize that the man in the dunk tank was a very-waterlogged Greg, who was still wearing the woman's dress he had on while stilt-walking through the fairway. His clown paint was nearly melted away, and his long-haired wig was drenched. He was taunting the poor kid throwing the ball, trying to trash-talk him into missing the target.

It worked, because when the kid threw his final ball, he missed.

"Ha ha!" Greg roared, slapping his knees as he sat on the platform. "You're all suckers! Every one of you! Don't see a single good arm among you."

Mia said, "Actually, he's pretty good at that. They're supposed to egg people on, make them want to take a chance. And now, even *I* want to hit him."

"You think he's good, you should see Johnny. He's the pro." He looked around. "Wonder where he is?"

Her smile slowly faded as his words registered. "What?"

"Johnny. That's his spot. On the platform. Always has been."

She gazed at the platform. Then she turned and looked at the Ferris wheel. And just like that, it all came together for her. Up on that platform, a person would have a perfect view of the ride, as it went around and around.

"Oh, my God," she whispered, rushing forward before she remembered she was wearing that annoying dress.

"Where are you going?" Will called as she stumbled forward.

She didn't answer. She grabbed the extra fabric and held it to her side as she ran forward, to the booth. Just as she did, someone hit the target and sent Greg splashing into the tank, sending a wall of water over the top of it, right onto her. It was briny and gross and slapped her in the face like a hand, leaving her stunned.

Blinking away the drops she pounded on the edge of the tank as Greg surfaced, wiping his hair out of his eyes. "Greg!"

"Hey, Rolanda! You want to take my place?" he said with a wink, grabbing the front of his dress and beginning to wring it out.

"No!" Palms flat against the plastic partition, she said, "Where's Johnny? Was he here?"

He eyed her with confusion as he reached for the platform, to get back into place. "Yeah, he was here. But Buck needed him. Why, what's going on?"

That was good news. If this hunch was right, and Johnny was the killer, Buck keeping him busy meant that he likely wasn't thinking of killing. "Where did Buck bring him? Do you know?"

"He needed him to operate a ride. Randy was sick and hadn't come back, so he told him to fill in." He pointed behind her. "The Ferris wheel."

She whirled around, wiping the water out of her eyes, searching for Johnny Rose.

That was when she heard the scream.

CHAPTER THIRTY

"That's it," Johnny Rose grunted as he looked up at the Ferris wheel. As he did, water from the dunk booth dripped off his nose. He brushed it back and took a deep breath. *Calm. Not yet. You can't do it yet.*

But a little voice inside him, growing ever louder, said, *Yes. You know you want to. So do it. Right now.*

Standing at the controls of the wheel, Johnny's hands shook. He had stopped the wheel with the teenagers' cart at the top, just as the kid had asked him to, while handing him a twenty and winking. It was the same young couple he'd been watching since earlier in the night. They'd ridden the wheel five times tonight—Johnny had counted, from his place on the platform of the dunk tank. Each time, the girl had looked more thrilled. She'd even gushed, "That's my favorite ride! I bet it would be awesome to see the fireworks from there!"

And so the kid in the football jersey had done everything in his power to make his love's dream come true. Just as Johnny would've done for his girl, Mary Violet.

Now, the number of riders had dwindled, and there was no line. Everyone had moved to the front of the fairgrounds in order to sit in the field and on the benches to watch the fireworks. So the area was relatively empty, and the teens' cart was one of only three full carts on the wheel. Johnny had helped the girl, with her arms full of stuffed animals into the cart, made sure the lap bar was fastened, and let them go.

Now, as he looked up, he saw the cart, above, in silhouette against the moonlit sky, rocking gently, back and forth.

Just as he thought. The boy was probably making the cart rock, so the girl would get nervous and cling to him. Soon, they'd be making out, under the fireworks.

How nice for them.

How perfect.

He gritted his teeth. It wasn't fair. It wasn't fair how these people could have this time. He hadn't. It'd been robbed from him, and no matter how many times he tried to move past it, he never did. He'd go his whole life without knowing what being with his true love was like.

And he hated anyone who had that opportunity. But most of all, he hated the people who flaunted that opportunity. Like these kids, here. Disgusting. So disgusting, he couldn't think straight.

His hands shook more than ever now, so much that he couldn't hit the switch to turn the ride back on now, even if he wanted to.

He stalked over to a nearby booth, where someone had left a metal pole, used to pull down stuffed animals from high-up places. Then he jogged back to the wheel and inserted the pole into the workings, wedging it in nice and deep. That would hold for a little while, in case they came after him. Long enough for him to do what needed to be done.

He reached into his pocket, pulling out a pocket knife. One of his hobbies in this business had been collecting weapons. Going place to place, acquiring them from underground sources. He'd left the gun at the last two places, making them think it was a murder-suicide, so he'd keep the police off his tail. But now, he didn't care.

Even if he got caught, which he likely would by that nosy woman, he couldn't help it anymore. He'd kill her, too. The pain inside him, from the boiling rage, was too much. He had to end this. Now. Before he went insane.

As he was gazing up at them, focusing all his growing rage at them, something whistled into the sky. Faraway, people gasped as it exploded and a spiderweb of pink filled the air. The first fireworks crackled in the sky above.

And Johnny Rose had had enough.

Jumping onto the platform at the base of the Ferris wheel, he grabbed ahold of the scaffolding and, ignoring the shouts of the people in the other carts and on the ground below, began to climb.

CHAPTER THIRTY ONE

As the first fireworks lit up the sky, Mia heard the screams, coming from the Ferris wheel.

She was already on her way there, past kiddy rides, though she still couldn't see what the commotion was about. When she rounded the face-painting tent, the first thing she saw was a number of people, standing frozen, staring at the ride.

When she followed the pointing fingers, she saw what had them so concerned. Someone was climbing the scaffolding of the wheel, making his way up to the very top of the wheel.

Mia could tell by black clothing that hugged his fit frame exactly who it was. It was Johnny Rose. "Oh, my God," she whispered, as nearby a woman let out a blood-curdling scream.

"Hell!" a voice said behind her. It was Will. "Is that Johnny? What is he up to?"

She scanned to the top of the wheel. Most of the carts were empty, but the one at the very top, the one that Johnny seemed to be angling toward, was rocking slightly. Full. As she strained in the dim light emanating from the fireworks and the lights on the side of the wheel, she could just see the forms of two people. She saw a hand reach out, pointing at a beautiful explosion in the sky.

Mia had been at the top of a Ferris wheel before, with Aiden. She knew what it was like, to be in love with someone and in that spot. It was entirely possible to feel like you were alone in the world, especially under a fireworks-filled sky. "They don't know what's going on," she whispered, mostly to herself.

That was bad. It meant they'd be completely unaware of the attack. Defenseless.

Rushing around frozen onlookers, she climbed the steps to the controls at the base of the wheel, two at a time. She stared at them, wondering which one to push. The red "STOP" button was depressed, but there was a green button that simply said "ON."

She jabbed at it. The wheel lurched, slightly, but did not move any farther. She pressed again. That time, nothing happened.

Will jogged up to see what she was doing. She kept jabbing. "Why isn't this working? Shouldn't it start the—do you know how to--?"

"Yeah," he said, pushing it, now, too. "It's not working. I think he might've jammed the controls somehow? I don't know. What the hell? What is he doing?"

She looked up. Johnny was more than halfway up, and getting closer. She cupped her hands around her mouth. "Johnny!"

He didn't even look down. She couldn't see his face, but he moved with determination. Something in him must've snapped, because he clearly didn't care about anyone else around him, watching him. He wasn't going to stop, not until he'd gotten what he'd come for.

He was going to kill them, whether or not he would get caught.

Will pointed into the gears. "Look. What is this thing?" He reached for a metal pole, sticking out of the workings. He tried to jiggle it, but it stayed put. "It's wedged in there. I think it's stopping the wheel from moving!"

She craned her neck to see upwards, the bright light from the attraction and the fireworks blurring her vision. "Up there! On the Ferris wheel!" She shouted, but her voice was drowned by the cheerful sounds of the music, the other rides, and the loud thunder of the fireworks.

Helplessly, she looked around, at her stupid dress. Grabbing the material, she tied it off to her side and looked for a path up. She found it, in a bit of zig-zag pattern, up the spokes of the wheel. "I'm going up."

"Are you crazy?" Will shouted, but she'd already found a foothold and had begun climbing after Johnny.

Despite the heat, the metal of the spokes was cold in her hands, sharp, not accustomed to being climbed. She scaled it, trying to remember back to the one rock-climbing class she'd taken with Aiden, when they were newlyweds. Aiden had been an expert, and he'd gently coached her through it. *Don't look down. Don't think too many steps ahead. Make sure each foot and hand is secure before you make your next step.*

When she was halfway up, almost even with the center of the wheel, she heard Will calling up to her. She made out one word. *Move!*

"What?" she called to him, still refusing to look down.

When he spoke again, he sounded louder, clearly enunciating every word: "*The. Pole. Won't. Hold! It's starting to bend!*"

Just as he finished those words, the wheel gave a sudden lurch forward. Her heart sped up and she wrapped her arms tightly to the spoke she'd been scaling. "Press the emergency stop!"

"I can't!" he shouted up to her. "It's not working!"

She heard the hollow clang of metal below her, and then suddenly, the wheel began to lurch again, violently. It stopped, stuttered, and started, sending all the carts rocking wildly. People in the carts began to scream.

Wrapping her arms around the metal spoke, she looked down. She was too far up to simply jump. Besides, she couldn't. As she looked up, she saw Johnny, still moving for the cart. The movement of the wheel had thrown him off-course, but now he was next to it, reaching for it. Mia watched helplessly as he took hold of the cart, holding it steady.

Then, suddenly, he dove for the cart.

Around her, people gasped. He managed to grab the edge of it and hold onto the side, clinging to the outside as he leered into it, at the passengers. The cart rocked. The girl began to scream, high-pitched and scared to death. "Help!"

As fast as she could, Mia grabbed for the next bar and pulled herself up. Then the next, and the next. She flew through them, tuning everything else out, and made it to the cart, which was now rocking wildly back and forth. She grabbed the first thing she could find up above, which happened to be Johnny's cowboy boot, and used it to hoist herself up.

Without warning, he wheeled on her and swiped the blade low, in her direction. She jerked back to avoid the slice, losing her hold on his leg, and dropped down, suddenly in a freefall.

Before she could even realize she was in trouble, she reached out, grabbing for whatever she could, and managed to hold onto a bar at the bottom of the cart. As she tried to hoist herself up, Johnny's face appeared, hanging over the edge, gazing at her with absolute hatred. "Get out of here!" he shouted, jabbing the knife in her direction.

She was just out of his reach, but she couldn't hold on to the bar for long. Her feet swung freely, wild, trying to find a foothold, but she was dangling without any help. "Johnny," she begged. "Think of what you're doing. Stop it."

He looked her straight in the eye, and in that moment, she saw nothing but madness. "No. Not until I'm done. And if you don't get the hell out of here, I'll kill you, too."

She slipped, losing her grip, and now it was only her fingers around the bar. "Johnny. Don't—"

"Drop, Rolanda," he commanded her.

She shook her head, scrabbling to get a better grip on the bar. Was he crazy? It was sixty feet to the ground, and the hard metal base of the Ferris wheel loomed below them. If she dropped, she'd die, anyway. "No."

He leaned over, and began to rock the cart back and forth, slowly at first, and then faster and faster. The motion was too much. She was quickly losing her hold on the bar, her clammy fingers growing numb.

An evil smile spread over his face, and he commanded once again, "Drop."

She could barely think. Could barely breathe. All of her strength was waning, and her hands, above her, were quickly losing all feeling. Around her, the colored lights blurred together like paint going down a drain, and the voices and screams of the people rose up from the ground, buffeting her eardrums. Sweat poured down her forehead, and into her eyes. She blinked it away.

"No," she said again. She wasn't going to die like this, no matter what. In that crazy rush, with her heartbeat pounding in her chest, she made a decision. She wouldn't give up without a fight.

So with her last bit of energy, Mia pulled herself up, letting out a groan of effort. She swiped her hand out, grabbing for his boot. She made contact and yanked, as hard as she could.

It was a last-ditch effort, and he had the high ground. She fully realized it was hopeless. And it wouldn't have done anything if not for the fact that, at that moment, the wheel lurched forward again.

He was still smiling, even as the motion knocked him off balance. And then, his eyes went wide.

She clung to the bar beneath the cart for dear life, closing her eyes, she didn't see him fall. She only heard his scream, all the way down, until the terrific crash of his body colliding on the platform below.

CHAPTER THIRTY TWO

Kane Wilcox turned up the AC in his car, letting the cold air blast his face.

He'd been driving since dinnertime, when he'd had the conversation with Momma in Canton. Three hours, and due to a traffic jam and a couple of slow-pokes, he still wasn't anywhere close to the Sabine Parish fairgrounds, which is where he expected to catch up with the carnival. He'd been exhausted, then, when he'd been eating, but the coffee and the lead had given him a second wind.

Now, though, that second wind was starting to leave him. He yawned and checked the dashboard clock—it was almost ten-thirty. The carnival ran until eleven. If he was lucky, he'd just make it there as the place was clearing out.

And he might be too late.

If he was even right in the first place. And that was a big *if*. Yes, the murders seemed to be following carnivals. But that didn't mean Mia was here.

But if Mia North was seriously pursuing this murderer, it meant that she'd be there. Now, under the cover of darkness, scoping the place out. She'd be so intent on finding her target, bringing him down, that she'd let her guard down.

And that's where he could swoop in and grab her.

At least, that was what he was hoping for.

And if that meant that the killer would get away, so be it. It wasn't his problem. Unlike Mia, he didn't care about the murderer that might or might not have been on the loose. He could've killed a thousand people to Mia's one. She was his number one target. Everything else was simply background noise.

He straightened and tightened his fingers around the steering wheel as he came to the sign that said, *NOW ENTERING MANY, LOUISIANA.*

Eventually, the darkness at the edge of town gave way to homes and a downtown area. He saw the first sign for the fairgrounds, pointing straight ahead. Pressing on the gas, he sailed straight through a yellow light that was about to turn red. Luckily, at this time of night, even the streets of downtown were empty.

As the lights of the town faded behind him, other lights came into view. Fireworks. They filled the sky, again and again, all colors, exploding upon a midnight blue canvas. As he drove his car away from the town, he saw them above the trees, and then, as he broke free of the forest, he saw the other lights, closer to the earth. The bright, many-colored lights of the carnival—the spinning carousel, the tall Ferris wheel, and other rides, all glowing cheerfully.

As he pulled up to the entrance to the fairground parking lot, he found himself in a maze of traffic, all attempting to leave the park. Wilcox was the only one trying to venture *in*, which they clearly hadn't expected, because they'd opened all lanes to let traffic out.

A man in an orange vest, alarmed, held out his hands to him. "Whoa, whoa, whoa!" the guy shouted as Wilcox powered down his window. "You can't go this way. You need to—"

"U.S. Marshal. I need to get in there, *now*," he said urgently, flashing his badge. "Is there an emergency route?"

The man in the orange vest quickly changed his tune. "Uh, yes sir. Right this way."

He motioned cars out of the way and directed Wilcox to the shoulder, where he mimed for him to do a U-turn. He jogged up to the window and pointed to a dark, grassy lane running parallel to the lot. "If you go around that way, you should be able to get in through the back."

Kane nodded. "Thanks."

He tore off, dipping into a ditch on the side of the road and pumping the gas. His tires squealed underneath him, trying to regain traction, before he lurched forward, bumping over the uneven terrain. Flooring the gas pedal, he drove wildly along an orange temporary fence, passing the tents and booths and rides in a blur as he made his way to the back entrance.

When he saw an opening, he punched the brakes, and his car groaned in protest underneath him. Throwing open the door and slipping out, he heard the screams.

He ducked through the fence and found himself in a utility area, with a number of dumpsters and trailers for the attractions. Rushing forward toward the crowd, he finally reached the fairway. Fireworks were exploding in the sky, and yet the people were not looking up above.

No, they were all staring, frozen in shock, at the Ferris wheel.

When Kane followed their line of vision, he could see why.

Two people were dangling from the top of it. As he watched the scene, dumbstruck as the rest of the crowd, one of the people—a man—lost his grip and fell backward, his body landing with a crash on the ground below. People screamed.

Somehow, I know Mia's behind this, he thought, breaking into a jog, never losing sight of the remaining person on the wheel. A woman, he could see. Smaller, with dark hair, blowing in the breeze, she somehow clung to the bottom of the topmost Ferris wheel cart.

Mia. It was Mia.

His heart leapt in his throat, as rush of energy overcame him. He dodged his way through the motionless people, finally approaching the base of the Ferris wheel. Cupping his hands around his mouth, he shouted, "Mia North!"

She looked down.

I've got her. I've finally got her.

"He's still alive!" someone shouted from the metal platform, a few steps above. There was a small group of people, gathering around the fallen man. "Is anyone a doctor? A nurse? Anything?"

People looked around, stupefied.

Kane stood there, looking from Mia to the injured man, hoping someone would come forward to help him. No one did. Mia was no longer looking at him. Instead, she was looking around wildly. *For escape.*

But she has no escape, he decided as she managed to lift herself up. A man inside the cart reached for her, helping her in. *I've got her.*

As he went to mind the injured man, he saw a teenaged boy and an older man, standing by the controls. They had the top off the panel, and the older man was furiously working with the electrical wires. "What's wrong, can't you get it to work?"

"No, the guy messed with it," the kid said, looking up. "Hang on, Ro!"

Ro? "You know her?"

The kid nodded. "Yeah, she works with us."

So that was it. She'd been working for the carnival, getting to know people. It made sense. Kane looked at the older man. "Can you get them down?"

"Doing the best I can," the older man muttered, not looking up from his work.

Mia would have to stay put for a while. He had time. Jogging to the injured man, he crouched in front of him. His leg was clearly broken, and likely his spine and a few other bones. But he was alive, gasping for air.

"Clear out," Kane said, motioning for everyone to stand back. "Let's give him some breathing room. Did anyone call 9-1-1?"

"I did," someone called. "On their way."

He got to work, clearing the injured man's airway, stabilizing him. As he hunched over, he heard footsteps around him, and then two men in blue uniforms appeared. The EMTs.

Kane stood up to let them take over, wiping the sweat from his brow, just as the man at the controls said, "Got it."

He rubbed his hands together. Good. In another minute, he'd finally have Mia North. He'd be able to talk to her, to finally get answers to the thousands of questions he'd amassed since this chase began.

Looking up, the fireworks display had ended, leaving nothing but gray smoke. He watched as the wheel spun and stopped, to let frightened guests off the ride. As they jumped out of the cart, he kept an eye on the one that held Mia, tapping his foot in anticipation.

"That was so scary!" a little girl cried as she stepped off the ride. "I never want to go to a carnival again, Mommy!"

He let out a short, mirthless laugh. He didn't blame her. That would've been harrowing for anyone, much less a child.

But then his eyes shifted up to Mia's cart, and alarm flooded in when he realized what was happening, a beat too late.

She was standing on the top of the cart, legs spread slightly for balance. Her eyes were focused on a nearby oak tree, the branches of which hung about five feet away from the path of the Ferris wheel.

"What the . . ." murmured under his breath. *She wouldn't attempt that. It'd kill her.*

But he'd been following Mia long enough to know that she never gave up without a fight. And she liked to take risks.

Oh, hell. She would.

He sucked in air and shouted, "Mia!"

Suddenly, she leapt, like Superwoman, grabbing ahold of a branch and swinging into the foliage, where she promptly disappeared.

"Shit!" he called, racing to the edge of the platform and launching himself off of it. He hit the ground hard, then raced off toward the tree line, where the bright carnival lights gave way to absolute darkness. "Mia! I just want to talk to you!"

Nothing. No sounds, except the slight rustle of the leaves, made from a barely-there breeze.

No. Hell no. I'm not going to get this close, only to lose her again. I refuse.

Every moment that passed felt like an eternity. She was slipping through his fingers. He dove into the trees, branches and leaves scratching at his face as he turned this way and that, alerted to even the smallest of sounds. Crickets chirped in his ears, and an owl cried out, but there was no sign of human life, anywhere. Grabbing his phone, her turned on the flashlight and shone it in all directions.

Nothing She was gone.

"Dammit!" he shouted, curling his hands into fists. "Goddammit!"

At that moment, he'd never missed his wife's smile and home cooking more.

*

Kane Wilcox strode the empty, quiet fairgrounds, thinking of Dana. He wanted to call her, to hear her voice, but it was after midnight. He could just imagine her, curled up in bed, a romance novel tented on her chest, conked out. She always fell asleep while reading.

Something told him he wouldn't be getting home to her in Corpus Christi anytime soon.

The man who'd fallen from the Ferris wheel was one John Rose. He was now at the Western Louisiana Medical Center, and was expected to pull through. Wilcox had been interviewing people, learning bits about him. He'd worked for the carnival for many years, was a nice guy. Friendly. Most people didn't have anything bad to say about him.

And yet, several witnesses had seen him attempt to attack and murder a couple of teenagers on the Ferris wheel. "It was like he'd just snapped," one of the other carnies had said.

It seemed that way. But had he "just" snapped, or did he have a long history of doing the same thing, at other carnivals? One thing was for sure—the police weren't going to let him go until they figured it out.

And once again, Mia North had disappeared like a vapor into the air.

He reached the trailer some of the other carnies had directed him to, and knocked on the door. "Kane Wilcox, U.S. Marshal," he called.

The door swung open. “Wilcox,” the ruddy-faced man said, shaking his hand. “The name’s Buck. I own FunTime. Come on in.”

As Wilcox stepped in, he could smell it—whiskey. A quick look at the empty bottle in the trash can beside the desk confirmed it. Buck had been getting drunk. It was practically coming out of his pores, which was probably why he stumbled before slumping into his chair.

“Uh . . . I’m sure you want to know about Johnny.”

He shook his head. He knew it was probably ridiculous that he’d concern himself with a woman who’d murdered one felon, when there was a serial killer in their midst, a man who’d likely killed many times that number. But his hunt for Mia had become less about the crimes, and more about the person. Mia North had become somewhat of a fairy tale in his mind, something too unbelievable to be real. He needed to interact with her, talk to her, to confirm who she was. “The police are looking into that.”

The man frowned and tipped his cowboy hat back. “What are you looking into, then? I’m not gonna get in trouble for this, am I? I employ people that most places won’t. I like to give people a second chance. But I don’t—”

He held up a hand, silencing him. “I don’t care about any of that. That’s someone else’s job. What I want to know about is Mia North.”

Buck frowned. “Who?”

Of course Mia would’ve used an alias. He couldn’t go by name. “A woman. Mid-length dark hair. Mid-thirties. Pretty. Petite. Thin. She was working for you. Might’ve gone by the name of Ro?”

His eyes sparked with recognition. “Right. Rolanda. The new girl. That ain’t her real name?”

“Yeah. What was—”

“Superwoman, some called her. She stopped a mugging last night. That was something.”

“A mugging?”

He nodded. “Yeah, she seemed to think she was Cagney and Lacey, all rolled up into one, if you ask me. She was never *actually* working, doing carnival stuff. Terrible Madame Zola. The worst. I’m a businessman. I need reliable workers to do the work and bring the money in. But she . . . nah. I would’ve fired her but I’m short workers.” He blinked hard, as if he was having trouble focusing. “What do you want her for? She in some kind of trouble?”

“She’s a wanted criminal. I wanted to talk to her.”

His eyes widened. "I didn't know. I swear I didn't." Then he slapped the desk. "I *am* gonna get in trouble for this. Aren't I?"

Kane shook his head slowly. "Like I said, I just wanted to talk to her. Have you got any idea where she might have been headed? Did she tell you anything about where she was going?"

He shook his head and picked up his phone. He pressed a button and spoke into the receiver. "Shirley? You have Rolanda there? Can you send her to my office?"

He hung up and held up a finger. "One second. Shirley's getting her. We'll get to the bottom of this."

Kane shook his head doubtfully. *Mia's long gone. We will most definitely not be getting to the bottom of this tonight.* "Did she say anything to you while she was working here? Where she'd come from? Where she was headed?"

"Not that I can remember." He leaned forward. "So she's a criminal? What did she do?"

"I can't discuss that."

He let out a short laugh. "Funny, and here we all thought she was some kind of hero. A criminal? Wow."

She might be one of those, too, he thought, as the door opened, and a woman with bright red hair popped her head in.

"Sorry, Buck," the woman said with a shrug. "I checked all over but she's gone. Will told me he thought she ran off into the woods, for some reason."

Buck gave her a confused look. "She probably knew I was pissed about the Madame Zola thing. Guess she's gone." He shrugged and looked at Kane with a *Sorry, can't help you* expression.

The woman held up a bag. "I brought her things, in case that could help you?"

Kane stood up and grabbed it. "I'll take that. Thanks for your help."

He headed back to his car and slipped into the front seat, setting Mia's worn bag on the front passenger seat. Slipping it open, he looked inside. *Well, Mia. You got away from me again. The least you can do is give me a consolation prize.*

He looked through the bag, finding dingy, wrinkled clothes, an overnight kit, all the expected things. Groaning, he got to the very bottom of the bag, feeling thoroughly defeated. What had he expected? A little note that said, *Come find me, I'll be waiting for you, right here!*

As he was about to give up, he *did* find a folded, crumpled sheet of paper. Not getting his hopes up, he carefully unfolded it, and read. It was a half-dozen locations throughout Texas, with two names, right afterwards. He scanned it, at first not understanding, but as he got to the end, it all became clear:

Canton, TX – Mari Powell and Tobias Maxwell

Lookout Point, TX – Kiki Redbone and Jason Delaney-Sawyer

He stared at it for a long time, then grabbed his phone and typed in the first name on the list, a girl named Lyndsey Walker, from Abilene.

She was a teenager, attending Abilene High. She and her boyfriend had been murdered during a date earlier that year. There were no suspects.

Wilcox went to FunTime Amusements' webpage. Sure enough, the carnival had passed through Abilene, at almost exactly the same time that the murders had occurred.

"Holy cow," he breathed, going one by one, through each name. Every one, a sob story, a murdered teenager whose parents were desperate for answers.

And now, they had them.

So even though he hadn't gotten what he'd come for, Mia North *had* given him a gift, after all.

EPILOGUE

Getting out of Louisiana proved harder than Mia thought it would be.

It wasn't easy going. She'd hitchhiked her way out of Many, wondering what to do. That last scrape had been way too close. She'd seen U.S. Marshal Kane Wilcox, at the bottom of the Ferris wheel platform. So she'd decided she would have to keep her head down, keep a low profile, as much as possible. That meant ditching the enormous, black satin antebellum dress. But everything she had was gone. All she'd had was her phone, in her pocket, with about eleven-percent charge.

Thank goodness for Francine. Though she was the last person Mia wanted to get in trouble, she'd realized she had no choice. The second Mia had called, Francine said that she would be right there.

She'd spent the night, sleeping on the cold ground, in the woods, and when she finally saw Francine the following afternoon, after hiding out in the woods like some animal, she felt cold, hungry, alone.

But the second Francine hugged her, all those feelings went away. "Nice dress," Francine quipped in her ear. She could always make Mia smile, even at the worst of times.

"Thank God," she said, relaxing into her arms. "I don't think I could do this without you."

"Well, I don't know how much longer I can do this for," Francine said, looking around as she beckoned Mia to her car. "The feds are really looking at me. That Marshal visited me, too, a few days ago. When you called, I made it look like I was going on a little vacation to the coast, and I think they bought it, but I don't think they'll buy it another time."

"That's okay," Mia said, climbing into the comfortable front seat of Francine's SUV. She was so tired, she almost fell asleep immediately, right there.

But then Francine said, "I got out a hotel room in a place north of here. I think you can take a shower. I have a thousand dollars for you, too. Plus, I spoke to a guy who's going to get you a car."

She gazed at her sister in pure admiration. "Thank you. You're a lifesaver." She shivered in the AC being pumped through the vents. "I tell you, I really thought I was done for last night. I got so close to being caught by that Marshal."

Francine drove straight ahead, not looking at her. "Mia . . . that's what I wanted to talk to you about. I know you're innocent. Everyone who loves you does. But you can't keep tempting fate like this. Maybe you need to give up whatever you're trying to do. It's too dangerous."

She stared at her sister. "What? You know I can't. Aiden, and Kelsey—"

"I know you want to get back to them. But sometimes you have to admit defeat. With this car and the money, you should just go. Dye your hair, change your appearance again, and cross the border to Mexico. You can easily do that. And then you can live. Instead of running from place to place, constantly on edge. You can't do that forever."

Mia couldn't believe Francine was saying such a thing. Of course, running off to Mexico sounded good to her. Francine didn't have a husband or kids. For her, leaving her old life behind would be easier. "Live? You really think I can live without my family?" She shook her head. "No. I can't do that."

She stayed silent for the rest of the ride, thinking. Yes, Francine, and the rest of her family only wanted what was best for her. And maybe they thought running away was best. But for whom? Not for Mia.

Maybe for them, though. Maybe if Aiden and Kelsey didn't have to worry about her, they could finally move on. Tears sprang to her eyes at the thought. This had to be hard on them. The not knowing. Maybe by disappearing forever, she would be doing them a favor?

They arrived at the motel, a sunny yellow strip of rooms not far from the highway, and Mia got out and went to the room, dying for a shower and to change into something other than that heavy, ugly black dress. As soon as she closed the door, though, she noticed a yellow envelope on the table.

She went to it. "What's this?"

"Oh," Francine said, rummaging through her suitcase. "I forgot to tell you. I spoke with your partner, David, before I left. He told me to bring you that. He was going to leave it in your spot, he said, but when I told him I was going, he asked me to give it to you."

Mia lifted it off the table and touched the flap gingerly, as if it were dangerous. "What is it?"

Francine was laying out a new set of clothes for Mia to wear. She shrugged. "Don't know. Why don't you open it and answer the question yourself?"

The much-needed shower forgotten, she lowered herself into the chair near the table and pulled open the flap. She lifted out a single sheet of paper, recognizing David's scrawled handwriting on a printout from the web. It looked like a web page from an escort service, with little avatars of scantily clad women with sexy names.

What on earth is this?

She pulled it out a little more and saw names like Kitty Lust and Sweetie Pye. David had circled the photograph of a young girl in pigtails and a short skit, and written next to it: *This is Lila Watkins, who was last seen over a year ago. Kevin Reynolds called to downtown Dallas Hyatt where she was staying with her "father."*

Mia stared at it, her eyes nearly bulging out of her head. Father?

Not on your life.

But was it Wilson Andrews she'd been shacked up with? There was no definite proof, but all signs pointed that way. Kevin Reynolds, who was now dead. Lila Watkins, an underage girl, missing. The Dallas Hyatt, where Wilson Andrews was known to spend a lot of his time.

Something was definitely not right here.

She noticed some more circles, of other women on the site. It turned out, Lila was not the only missing escort. There were four, in all, missing from Dallas in the past year. Likely, they were people without families, runaways, people who could easily go missing, without anyone ever suspecting a thing.

Wilson Andrews was responsible, at least in some way. Either he'd been involved, or he knew who was. She just knew it.

And if anyone was going to hold his feet to the fire for it and make him confess to all the dirty things he'd done, she wanted to be that person.

An idea struck. She sucked in a breath, and let it out. Dangerous, foolhardy, explosive. Could she do it?

It would be risky, all or nothing. But she could end it all, right now.

She thought of Aiden and Kelsey, and her heart twisted. Yes, she decided, she could. She *would*.

*

Mia knew the office of Wilson Andrews well.

In another life, when she'd been an FBI agent and everything was normal, she used to pass by his building, every day. It was an investment firm, a stately brick building with a fountain out front and a giant American flag on one side, the Texas flag on the other. The landscaping was always immaculate, with colorful flowers bursting up at all times of year, and the parking lot was always filled with impressive luxury cars—not just the standard Lexus and Mercedes, but McLarens and Bugatti, too. She didn't care much for cars, but every time she'd pass the lot with David, he'd whistle and say, "Whew, would you look at that sweet ride?"

She was easily able to sneak in. They had cameras everywhere, but no one was manning them. There was a big party going on in the main lobby, downstairs, for all the firm's many clients. She'd done plenty of research, so she knew that tomorrow was a big day of presenting to a college campus, so he'd have to get up early and likely wouldn't try to find any "company" for the evening. She also knew, from rumors, that he was a superstitious man who never left the building until he'd had his glass of scotch. He'd said in *Forbes,* once: "The last time I left the building without that scotch was March 16, 2020, and we all know what happened that day," referring to the enormous stock market crash. Pretending to be security, she'd worn a face like she belonged there and easily slipped in, unnoticed.

Now, the party was winding down. Wilson's fun time was over.

Hers was just beginning.

As she stood in his dark office, looking around the vast, immaculate space full of polished mahogany and rich burgundy leather, oozing wealth, privilege, and masculinity, something caught in her throat. In a dim shaft of moonlight, shining through a skylight overhead, she spied the Harvard diploma on the wall, the photographs on his massive desk of him rubbing shoulders with celebrities and dignitaries.

He had every advantage in life. He'd been given everything from a young age. She couldn't fault people for that. But what did make her sick to her stomach was the way he'd used those advantages to further his sick desires. Even when Wilson Andrews did wrong, he could do no wrong. He always had a safety net to prop him up, no matter what evil things he was a part of. The same had been true of Jerry, his brother, who'd kidnapped young girls and treated them like his personal playthings. Other people were only there to satisfy the Andrews boys' wants—they were disposable.

Mia had been disposable, too. So no matter what happened to her, no matter how much she was tortured, it wouldn't matter to him. He would never feel remorse.

She swallowed the bitter taste in her mouth. She'd never been one to hate anyone. But Wilson Andrews? She hated him. So much, she shook with fury as she stood in his office.

Calm down, Mia. Calm yourself. You're no good to anyone if you're blinded by rage.

As she stood there, behind his desk, she took a cleansing breath. Then another.

She heard the footsteps and clenched her fists at her sides as the door to the office opened. Wilson Andrews's substantial, broad form filled much of the space in the doorway as he fumbled for the light. He swayed a little, suggesting the scotch he'd soon pour himself was probably not his first alcoholic beverage of the night.

She blinked in the bright light from the banker's lamp on his desk, taking in his form. He was mid-fifties, fit except for a little belly, and he had a full head of salt-and-pepper hair that he usually swept back from his face. Always dressed in an expensive custom suit, photos of him as a young man had him looking like a young Alec Baldwin; but the years of drinking and who-knew-what-else had aged him significantly, from the broken blood vessels on his nose to the doughy, uneven, unhealthy pallor of his skin.

He didn't look her way. He simply toddled over to the mini-bar, loosening his bow tie. With his back to her, she heard him pop ice cubes into the glass and pour his drink from a fancy decanter.

Mia took a deep breath. It was time.

"I thought you were more of a neat scotch drinker," she said.

He whirled, his drink sloshing over the lip of the glass, onto his hand. "Jesus!" he shouted at her, looking down at the mess he'd made. "What the hell? How the hell did you get in . . ."

He stopped as recognition dawned on his face. His mouth fell open, and it was a full five seconds before he said, "You're that woman. That agent. Mia North."

She smirked. "I'm surprised. You actually know my name. You should, since you did me the favor of completely destroying my life."

He took a long, slow sip of his drink and swallowed. "You expect me to feel sorry? After what you did to my brother?"

She shrugged. "He is a murderer. A felon. Just like you."

He drained the rest of the drink and set it down. "I have no idea what you're talking about. But I do know that you're wanted for murder. You're very in-demand, it seems, among your former law-enforcement friends. So what do you say I go ahead and help them out?"

He advanced toward the phone on his desk. She moved between him and it. Shaking his head, he reached into his pocket and pulled out his cell phone.

"I know about the girls. Kitty Lust. Lila Watkins. And all the others. I know that you were with them, and now they're missing."

His surprised morphed into amusement. "What do you know? Whatever it is, you can't prove a damn thing. And I don't know a damn thing you're talking about."

"You had Kevin Reynolds killed because he could've identified you as the person who was with Lila Watkins that night. I bet he even knows what you did with her."

"You're talking nonsense, girl." He looked up at the ceiling.

"Kevin Reynolds. The policeman. He's the same one you had set it up to make it look like I killed Ellis Horvath. You had me framed." She didn't like his smug smile. He looked so untouchable, like nothing could break through his suit of armor, so she added the lie: "I have proof."

"You do, now?" He didn't buy it.

She nodded. "When you had your boy kill Reynolds, you didn't know he felt guilty about the whole Lila Watkins thing, not reporting it. He wrote and signed a confession, implicating you. And I have it. Somewhere very safe."

The smile disappeared. Now, for the first time, he looked—not necessarily worried. People like Wilson Andrews didn't worry. There was always an out for them. But he definitely looked angry. He played with people's lives, but he didn't like being played with himself.

"Where do you have it?"

She smiled.

He advanced on her. "Where do you have it?"

She held her ground, not flinching, even as he came up close to her. She simply said, "That's for me to know, and you will only find out when it's blasted across every news channel in the country."

His scowl deepened. "What do you want? In exchange for your silence? Name your price."

As much as she tried not to let it waver, her voice cracked when she thought of everything she'd lost. "I want my life back."

"Can't do that," he said, looking down. "You know that."

"I don't. You have all the power. There's got to be something you can do. Find a way to get all charges against me dropped, and I swear . . . I'll keep your secrets, until the day I die. I promise that."

He smiled and tutted a little, shaking his head as he paced, hands behind his back, around her. This time, she let him go to his desk where he sat down in his chair and pulled himself under it. "Now, how am I supposed to believe you?"

"I want to be with my family again. More than anything," she said, practically shaking from the desire.

He laced his fingers together and propped them under his chin. "Really. But I've been hearing rumors about you. Rumors that, even while on the lam, you've been meddling in cases that don't involve you. Out of the goodness of your heart. You're like a real superhero, a wanted fugitive who solves cases in her spare time. Everyone's talking about it. They think that despite being caught for your own crime, you simply can't see injustice without wanting to act on it."

Mia took in his words, hardly able to believe they were true. People were talking about her? Rumors were flying around that she was some kind of anti-hero? David and Francine had never told her that. All she ever knew as far as public opinion was what she'd read in the paper—that she was a dangerous criminal, on the run from the law.

"Is that true?" he asked her.

She didn't confirm or deny. She'd never thought of herself in those terms. She was just doing what she had to do.

"Because I find it very hard to believe that someone with such a sense of justice would turn a blind eye to the case of Lila Watkins. To simply walk away."

His smile widened, and her breath caught. He was right. As much as she wanted to be with Aiden and Kelsey, she couldn't read about cases like Lila Watkins, knowing who was responsible for her disappearance, and do nothing. It wasn't in her blood to sit idly by while criminals got away.

So she said nothing.

This was a mistake, she realized as she stood there. She should've planned it better, amassed real evidence, instead of letting her heart lead her in here. Now, she felt foolish, off-kilter. "I guess I'll give the information I know about you to the local news, then," she began. "Because they will—"

She stopped when she heard it. Sirens. Coming closer.

Mia gazed at him with growing horror as he pointed underneath the desk. "A panic button. It comes in handy in my line of work," he said, that smug smile returning, full-force.

She whirled to the window, where she saw the red and blue lights of the police cars, pulling into the roundabout near the fountain. It looked like at least two cars, maybe more. Of course, the police catered to their best citizen, the esteemed Wilson Andrews.

And she was nothing but a criminal.

Spinning helplessly, she could do nothing but back up against the corner. She'd made her share of rash, stupid mistakes since going out on the lam. But she had a feeling that this one was the worst of them.

Because now, she was trapped.

NOW AVAILABLE!

<u>SEE HER GONE</u>
(A Mia North FBI Suspense Thriller—Book 5)

FBI Agent Mia North remains a fugitive, on the run for a crime she didn't commit—when an old prison friend begs for her help solving a case of a killer that has murdered her family—and others—in a string of trailer parks. As the case broadens to something diabolical, Mia may find herself face to face with a killer without any backup.

"A brilliant book. I couldn't put it down and I never guessed who the murderer was!"
—Reader review for Only Murder

Special Agent Mia North is a rising star in the FBI—until, in an elaborate setup, she's framed for murder and sentenced to prison. When a lucky break allows her to escape, Mia finds herself a fugitive, on the run and on the wrong side of the law for the first time in her life. She can't see her young daughter—and she has no hope of returning to her former life.

The only way to get her life back, she realizes, is to hunt down whoever framed her.

Can she find and stop the killer—and figure out who framed her—before she herself is caught by the U.S. Marshals?

An action-packed page-turner, the MIA NORTH series is a riveting crime thriller, jammed with suspense, surprises, and twists and turns that you won't see coming. Fall in love with this brilliant new female protagonist and you'll be turning pages late into the night.

Book #6 in the series—SEE HER DEAD—is now also available.

"I loved this thriller, read it in one sitting. Lots of twists and turns and I didn't guess the
culprit at all… Already pre-ordered the second!"
—Reader review for Only Murder

"This book takes off with a bang… An excellent read, and I'm looking forward to the next book!"
—Reader review for SEE HER RUN

"Fantastic book! It was hard to put down. I can't wait to see what happens next!"
—Reader review for SEE HER RUN

"The twists and turns kept coming. Can't wait to read the next book!"
—Reader review for SEE HER RUN

"A must-read if you enjoy action-packed stories with good plots!"
—Reader review for SEE HER RUN

"I really like this author and this series starts with a bang. It will keep you turning the pages till the end of the book and wanting more."
—Reader review for SEE HER RUN

"I can't say enough about this author! How about 'out of this world'! This author is going to go far!"
—Reader review for ONLY MURDER

"I really enjoyed this book… The characters were alive, and the twists and turns were great. It will keep you reading till the end and leave you wanting more."
—Reader review for NO WAY OUT

"This is an author that I highly recommend. Her books will have you begging for more."
—Reader review for NO WAY OUT

Rylie Dark

Bestselling author Rylie Dark is author of the SADIE PRICE FBI SUSPENSE THRILLER series, comprising six books (and counting); the MIA NORTH FBI SUSPENSE THRILLER series, comprising six books (and counting); the CARLY SEE FBI SUSPENSE THRILLER, comprising six books (and counting); and the MORGAN STARK FBI SUSPENSE THRILLER, comprising three books (and counting).

An avid reader and lifelong fan of the mystery and thriller genres, Rylie loves to hear from you, so please feel free to visit www.ryliedark.com to learn more and stay in touch.

BOOKS BY RYLIE DARK

SADIE PRICE FBI SUSPENSE THRILLER
ONLY MURDER (Book #1)
ONLY RAGE (Book #2)
ONLY HIS (Book #3)
ONLY ONCE (Book #4)
ONLY SPITE (Book #5)
ONLY MADNESS (Book #6)

MIA NORTH FBI SUSPENSE THRILLER
SEE HER RUN (Book #1)
SEE HER HIDE (Book #2)
SEE HER SCREAM (Book #3)
SEE HER VANISH (Book #4)
SEE HER GONE (Book #5)
SEE HER DEAD (Book #6)

CARLY SEE FBI SUSPENSE THRILLER
NO WAY OUT (Book #1)
NO WAY BACK (Book #2)
NO WAY HOME (Book #3)
NO WAY LEFT (Book #4)
NO WAY UP (Book #5)
NO WAY TO DIE (Book #6)

MORGAN STARK FBI SUSPENSE THRILLER
TOO LATE (Book #1)
TOO CLOSE (Book #2)
TOO FAR GONE (Book #3)

www.ingramcontent.com/pod-product-compliance
Lightning Source LLC
Chambersburg PA
CBHW030614310726
48979CB00003B/715

* 9 7 8 1 0 9 4 3 9 5 1 5 9 *